AND
THEN
THE SKY
EXPLODED

AND
THEN
THE SKY
EXPLODED

David A.
Poulsen

DUNDURN
TORONTO

Editor: Shannon Whibbs
Design: Laura Boyle
Cover design: Laura Boyle
Cover image: © Armin Staudt/ istockphoto.com
Printer: Webcom

Library and Archives Canada Cataloguing in Publication

Poulsen, David A., 1946-, author

    And then the sky exploded / David A. Poulsen.

Issued in print and electronic formats.

ISBN 978-1-4597-3637-5 (paperback).--ISBN 978-1-4597-3638-2 (pdf).--
ISBN 978-1-4597-3639-9 (epub)

    I. Title.

PS8581.O848A83 2016   jC813'.54   C2016-902247-1
                                    C2016-902248-X

1 2 3 4 5   20 19 18 17 16

We acknowledge the support of the **Canada Council for the Arts** and the **Ontario Arts Council** for our publishing program. We also acknowledge the financial support of the **Government of Canada** through the **Canada Book Fund** and **Livres Canada Books**, and the **Government of Ontario** through the **Ontario Book Publishing Tax Credit** and the **Ontario Media Development Corporation**.

Care has been taken to trace the ownership of copyright material used in this book. The author and the publisher welcome any information enabling them to rectify any references or credits in subsequent editions.

                                           — *J. Kirk Howard, President*

The publisher is not responsible for websites or their content unless they are owned by the publisher.

Printed and bound in Canada.

VISIT US AT
Dundurn.com | @dundurnpress | Facebook.com/dundurnpress | Pinterest.com/dundurnpress

Dundurn
3 Church Street, Suite 500
Toronto, Ontario, Canada
M5E 1M2

To Lee Spice — whose wisdom, insight, and compassion are an endless inspiration.

This is our cry. This is our prayer. Peace in the World.
— Sadako Sasaki's monument inscription, Hiroshima

August 6, 1945

Yuko hated eight o'clock in the morning.

Every day, whether there was school or not, Yuko's mother shook her awake at exactly eight o'clock. This day was no different. Even though it was August 6th and even though August 6th was Yuko's birthday.

"Rise up, Yuko, and greet the morning sun. Bed is for lazy, flop-eared dogs. The world awaits those who leap from their beds and run to meet it."

Yuko's mother said those words, or words very similar to those, every morning. Yuko didn't bother to answer. Instead she rubbed her eyes, yawned, and pushed back the covers.

Her mother stopped at the door, turned back to Yuko and smiled. "Happy birthday, Yuko."

Yuko smiled back at her mother, spun on her bed and dropped her feet into the slippers that were in the same place they always were, where she had left them the night before as she climbed into bed at the end of what had been a long, tiring day.

Yuko's smile disappeared and she groaned as she re-membered that this day would be the same as yesterday and the day before and the day before that. She and all her friends from the Keiko Hiroshima Prefectural Girls' School would be out in the streets helping to tear down buildings that could block the way of people needing to move about if American bombs were to rain down on the city.

The work was back-breaking and never-ending. Every time one building was down and the cleanup completed there was another ... and another. It wasn't the way Yuko wanted to spend her eleventh birthday.

Yuko was careful to wear the same clothes she had worn the day before, her summer school uniform. Even though her mother had washed it last night, it was far from clean. It would never be *really* clean again. But she would wear it again today. There was no point getting another of her summer school uniforms filthy. All of her classmates had taken to re-wearing the same clothes day after day for the same reason.

The girls had sewn the uniforms themselves and had been very proud of them at the time. Now they were unpleasant reminders of a war that it seemed would go on forever. And of the bombs that everyone said would one day target Hiroshima just as they had so many other Japanese cities.

Yuko washed her hands and face in the basin that sat next to her bed, then pulled on the uniform, the once new shimmer of the almond-brown fabric now the dull-ness of spring mud. She smoothed her hair with both hands and stared out of her room toward her brother

Kiyoshi's bedroom. It was much smaller than her own, Yuko had often thought with pride.

Her waking of her brother was another of the things that happened every single morning at exactly the same time. Eight-fifteen. Yuko sometimes wondered unhappily about why her brother got to sleep a quarter of an hour longer than she did.

But today she didn't think about that. Or even about the work that was ahead of her. Instead she wondered if there would be a present waiting for her when she got to the kitchen. Even in these war years when things had been difficult for Yuko's family, her mother had never failed to have something sitting on the table for her or her brother on birthday mornings.

Would today be the same?

As she moved down the narrow hall to her brother's room, her slippers making a gentle swishing on the wooden floor, she happened to glance out the window that faced the west.

At that exact instant a blinding flash — the light of a thousand thousand suns — tore apart the sky above the city.

And Yuko's world would never be the same.

PART 1

THE SECRET

CHAPTER
ONE

It was hot in the church. Hot and sticky. Uncomfortable. I was wishing I were somewhere else.

I guess I shouldn't call it a church. It was a funeral home. The building looked sort of like a church on the outside but inside there were no church services — just funerals.

I'd always figured funerals were all about sad — with mourners looking sad, and the minister looking sad, and the people who worked in the funeral home, all in dark suits and serious, sad faces.

And, of course there's the deceased. Which is why everybody is sad. Someone has died — the deceased. I had already learned it's better to say "the deceased" than to use any phrase that has the word *dead* in it. People don't like that, especially the mourners. At this funeral I was one of the mourners.

It was my first funeral. I'd managed to get all the way to fourteen years old, well, almost fourteen, without having to watch someone I knew be buried. But that all came to an end on October 16, 2015. My great-grandfather had died five days before — October 11 — same day as my sister Carly's birthday. She was fifteen — one year and twenty-two days older than me.

But since my great-grandpa had died that morning we didn't do much birthday celebrating, which Carly was totally bummed about. I was okay with the no-celebration part because it meant one less day of the year that I had to pretend to like my sister. The other ones were Christmas and Thanksgiving. Christmas makes sense, I guess — you're supposed to be nice to *everybody* on Christmas Day.

But I could never figure out Thanksgiving. Mom says it's the day we're supposed to be thankful for all of our blessings. And I don't have a problem with that. It's just that I don't consider Carly a blessing. Actually the best year was the one when my sister's birthday and Thanksgiving were the same day. Cut out exactly one third of the "be-nice-to-Sis" days.

That was back when we lived in Canada, where Thanksgiving is a lot earlier than here in America.

I was hoping that this year we'd just blow off Carly's birthday altogether, but no luck. I mean even Carly could sort of understand that it wasn't really appropriate to have a party with cake and candles and girls taking selfies on the day Great-Grandpa Will died. But Mom promised Carly that we'd celebrate her birthday a couple of weeks later.

We called him GG Will which is a lot simpler than Great-Grandpa Will, especially if you had to say it a whole bunch of times in a row.

William Deaver — that was his real name. He was my mom's grandpa. He had been a scientist and a professor and was the smartest person I'd ever met. He was also the coolest ninety-six-year-old guy in the world. How many guys on their ninety-third birthday are out there playing street hockey with their great-grandkids? Of course, he mostly played goal and we all maybe took it a little easy when we were shooting at his net. But he was out there laughing and having fun and even yelling at everybody on his team. He made a couple of pretty good saves, too.

I was remembering that day playing street hockey and some other stuff about GG Will while I was sitting there in the funeral place. Since I didn't have any actual experience with funerals, I didn't really know how to act. Lots of people around me were crying. I didn't cry. Not because I wasn't sad, I was. Like I said I really liked GG Will and I knew I was going to miss his jokes and his grilled-cheese sandwiches, which were unbelievable. He cooked them in tinfoil with an iron. Seriously.

And he could explain stuff that was totally complicated, but when he was done explaining, you understood it. I guess that was connected to how smart he was. Although I've known some pretty smart people who explain something and they finish and look at you like *you get it now, right*? And the whole thing is still a mystery. So I'll miss that about my GG Will. And his goaltending, I'll miss that, too.

Mostly I tried not to move around a lot. I figured fidgeting and turning around to look at the people behind me would have my sister tapping my mom on the arm and pointing at me: *Look at Christian, Mom. Can you make him stop acting like a child?* Or something like that. And then Mom would tell Dad and there'd be *the lecture* when we got home and I hated *the lecture* almost as much as I hated zucchini.

So I tried to look around without moving anything other than my head and eyes. I was sitting next to the window but when I tried to look out, the light was hitting the glass kind of funny and mostly what I saw was me … looking back at me.

Looking at myself is not one of my favourite pastimes. I know kids are supposed to be all about themselves and I guess I'm like that sometimes, but I just don't like looking at myself. In the morning, I try to get the face-washing, the teeth-brushing, and the hair-combing done with as little time as possible spent looking into the mirror.

But there I was in the reflection in the window of the funeral home. All five-foot-seven (170 cm) one hundred and twenty-two pounds of me, the same brown hair and brown eyes that had been me for thirteen years and eleven-plus months. So how would I describe my looks? Well, the word *handsome* wouldn't be part of the description, but I don't think *ugly* would either. Somewhere in between, I guess.

It wasn't a friendly face looking back at me from that window glass. I looked like I did most of the time — sort of pissed off at the world. Which I wasn't, not really, but some kids have happier looks on their faces, not that they're grinning or even smiling all the time, they just look like they're sort of okay with the way life is going.

That's not Christian Larkin. Even though my life is fine (if you don't count Carly), my brain doesn't seem to be able to convince my face of that. I try. Seriously, some mornings I tell myself *okay, today I'm all about happy* and I walk around smiling the whole time, but at the end of the day I feel like an idiot and my cheek muscles hurt. So I don't do that very often. It's easier to just be the guy the window glass said I was.

GG Will was inside a casket that was sitting right at the front of the centre aisle of the funeral home. We were in the right-hand rows, also at the front. Which meant we were right next to the casket. That's where the family sits at most funerals, which is one of the things I learned that day.

There were a couple of songs — hymns I guess — and the minister talked about Jesus, the shepherd, and how every sheep in the flock mattered to the shepherd. There was more but I didn't get all of it.

Up to then I hadn't been paying much attention to what was going on. I'd been watching this banner flutter high up on the wall at the front of the building, right over where the minister was standing. The banner had symbols on it and I'd been trying to figure out what the symbols meant and also why the banner was fluttering. It's not like there was a wind inside the funeral home.

I'd also been thinking about the smell, which was sort of strange, too. Actually a few smells together. Kind of a smell mix. There was the smell of coffee, which made sense since we'd all been in this waiting room until it was time to go into the main part of the building where the funeral was and there had been coffee in that room.

And there was the smell of soap and hair stuff and new clothes — like everybody had tried to be really clean and smelling okay — I figured that made sense too.

What didn't make sense was the other smell. It was popcorn. Who brings popcorn to a funeral? The answer is nobody, so where did the smell come from? It's not like there was a theatre next door. Actually there was a paint store on one side and a parking lot on the other. Neither of those is famous for popcorn.

So that was it — coffee and soap and popcorn. Or something that wasn't popcorn but smelled like popcorn. And there a couple of other smells that I didn't recognize right off.

Then my Uncle Eugene got up and talked about GG Will. I quit thinking about the banner and the smells and paid attention to Uncle Eugene. He was my mom's brother and GG Will's only grandson (there were a lot of girls in the family). The first couple of minutes he seemed to be having some trouble and was getting choked up, but then he got rolling and talked about GG Will's life in Canada and his work in the field of materials physics.

This part was hard to understand but mostly it sounded like GG Will was amazingly intelligent and his work in the field of nanostructures while he was teaching at McGill University in Montreal was groundbreaking. That's what Uncle Eugene called it. He went into some detail but I didn't understand a lot of it. *Any* of it, actually. See, that's where we needed GG Will explaining nanostructures so people like me could understand it.

Then Uncle Eugene got to the good part. He talked about how Great-Grandpa Will was more than just a brilliant scientist … how he loved to laugh and play tricks on people — like this one time at Halloween back when it sounded like Halloween was a lot more fun than it is now.

GG Will built this coffin-looking thing and dressed up like Dracula and all that night he'd lie in the coffin and when kids came to the house trick-or-treating, my Great-Grandma Molly would bring them into the front hall where they could see the coffin. Then just as the kids were getting their treats, GG Will would sit up in the coffin and start looking around like he was deciding which neck to bite. He only did that one year because it scared the crap out of some of the littler kids. Some parents phoned and complained. One guy even said he'd go to the cops if they did again the next Halloween. Uncle Eugene said it was GG Molly who put a stop to it. GG Will would have had that coffin out there again, cops or no cops.

I looked over at GG Will's coffin — the one he was in now — and I was wishing he could sit up right then and scare the crap out of some people and then we'd go outside and play some ball hockey. I knew it wasn't going to happen but it was sort of a cool thought.

It seemed like a long funeral but since it was my first one I didn't have a whole lot to compare it to. But finally two of the guys in dark suits came and wheeled the casket to the back of the place and we started getting up and following them outside. The family, we went first. A lady was playing the organ but I could still hear some people crying — just softly — here and there in the funeral home.

Once we got outside I figured we'd all get in cars and head out to the cemetery where some more stuff would happen at the gravesite. I knew this because Carly — the world's greatest expert on everything — had told me.

And I guess that's what would have happened if it hadn't been for the people with the signs.

I didn't see them at first because coming out of the funeral home into the bright sunshine — I was sort of blinded and couldn't really see much of anything. Actually I heard them before I saw them. You couldn't really *not* hear them since they were yelling.

One guy was hollering, "Murderer ... mass murderer!" every few seconds. I didn't get some of what they were yelling but I heard a girl screaming, "Women, old people, babies, you got them all ... good riddance to the butcher."

At first I figured it was weird that there was some kind of protest going on across the street from the funeral home. Except that once my eyes got used to the bright sunshine I realized the protest wasn't about some vet clinic that was doing medical experiments using white rats ... or an army recruiting centre ... or some political decision.

No, the protest wasn't about any of those things.

It was about us.

There were eight or maybe ten people, most of them looked about twenty or so — mostly guys but a couple of girls too.

Even though they were on the opposite side of the street the signs were big enough that I could read them. One said, KILLER OF THOUSANDS and another one said AUGUST 6, 1945, DAY OF SLAUGHTER.

A couple of people who worked at the funeral home were crossing the street to try to talk to the protesters. The rest of us just stood there, everybody kind of confused and not sure what to do next. That's when the cops arrived, three car loads, lights flashing but no sirens. We watched for a couple of minutes as the cops gathered up the protesters and shoved them in the back of a van that arrived right after the squad cars.

It was over pretty fast but the whole time the protestors were climbing in the van — they didn't fight at all which was probably smart — they kept yelling.

"Executioner," "Deaver the Bomb Builder," "Baby Killer," and a bunch of other stuff. The one I remember most was "Rest in peace my ass." I remembered it but I didn't get it. None of it.

The police van drove off followed by the police cars. Then the funeral home people eased GG Will's casket into the back of the hearse and we climbed into cars and headed for the cemetery. I noticed my dad had been standing between GG Molly and the protesters, like he was trying to block her from seeing them.

No one spoke all the way to the cemetery. Or even after we got there. While we were standing around the grave where GG Will would be placed after we were gone, I looked around at all the people who were standing there. Everyone had their heads down looking at the dirt or the grass that was just starting to turn brown after the long hot summer and fall.

When the casket had been lowered part way down, a couple of shovelfuls of dirt were dropped down on top of it. What my English teacher, Mrs. Gillingham, would call symbolism. Or maybe it was synecdoche … I always had trouble with that one.

The drive home was almost as quiet as the one to the cemetery. And that was it. My first funeral was over. I wouldn't forget it … ever.

And I knew there were some things I'd have to ask about.

CHAPTER
TWO

It was a couple of days before I started asking.

I guess I was almost afraid to. Maybe afraid of what I'd find out. Maybe afraid I'd make people mad by asking. But then I realized I had a right to know. I had a right to know why protestors were at my GG Will's funeral and why television and newspaper people kept calling the house trying to ask my mom and dad questions (my sister and I weren't allowed to answer the phone for several days).

And most of all I had a right to know why everybody was walking around like they'd had their tongues cut out and couldn't talk. It was like it is at school when somebody knows something and doesn't want to tell you so they don't talk to you at all … about anything. Like mentioning the Mariners game or what your parents sent for lunch that day would somehow cause the big secret to slip out.

I asked my mom first. I figured she'd be less likely to get mad and might actually tell me something. And besides, GG Will had been *her* grandfather.

I was wrong. It was like a rerun of *The Brady Bunch*. She actually said, "Ask your father." *Seriously? Ask your father?*

"Mom, this is crazy," I told her. "A bunch of people show up at a funeral of someone from our family and yell a bunch of nasty stuff and wave these signs around and now it's like I went to sleep and woke up in a silent movie. Why won't somebody talk to me?"

Mom was taking things out of the dishwasher and sticking them in cupboards and drawers. For a minute it didn't look like she was going to stop. Or even slow down. Then she did. She turned and looked at me.

"Chris, you have every right to want to know about your great-grandpa. The truth is I don't know all of it even though I'm his granddaughter. Your dad is more on top of that kind of thing than I am. It really would be best to talk to him."

"What kind of thing?"

"What?"

"You said Dad was more on top of this kind of thing. What kind of *thing* are we talking about?"

She turned back to the dishwasher. "Please, Christian … ask your dad."

"And will he actually tell me anything?"

She didn't answer right away. "I think he will," she said finally, but I noticed she was still almost hiding in the dishwasher.

"Mom, was GG Will, like, a serial killer or something? I mean you hear about families with these deep dark secrets and …"

She turned back to me again.

"Your great-grandfather wasn't a serial killer. He never killed *anyone*." She emphasized that last word like it was really important.

"Then what —"

She held up her hands to stop me.

"That's it. Talk to your dad … okay?"

I looked at her for a while before I answered.

"Okay." I nodded. "Okay."

"And now you can put away the cutlery," she said and headed for the stairs to the second level. That's the thing about living in a four-level split. There are lots of places people can hide. Mom was headed for one of them now.

Conversation over.

This four-level split sits in a cul-de-sac in Lake Arlington, one of Trimble's semi-old, semi-cool neighbourhoods. My dad is a vice-principal at Anna Fernicola Middle School — the one Carly and I both went to which meant he was our vice principal, which Carly and I agreed (one of the few times *that* happened) totally sucked.

Vice-principals are supposed to be good communicators. And maybe they are when they've got a skinny, scared fifth grader in the office and they're giving the kid a lot of crap for hitting some other kid in the back of the head with a snowball.

But sharing secrets about family members? Yeah, not so much.

For the first couple of days Dad played the "I'm busy, not right now" card. Made sure he had his laptop open and on whenever I was around. That way he could make it look like he was inputting kids' marks or sending vitally important emails and stuff. Couldn't *possibly* be interrupted.

My dad isn't like that normally. Three years ago when we moved to Trimble from Saskatoon, Saskatchewan, Dad was the go-to guy for all our questions about the state of Washington. In fact, pretty much the whole United States. He was a regular tourist promoter ... *you guys are going to love it there — it's a better climate, we'll be closer to great skiing, closer to your grandparents, there are lots of horse stables* (a big deal for Carly), *and we're one hour away from the Seattle Seahawks* (a big deal for me). But that didn't stop Carly and me from being totally unhappy about leaving Saskatoon. I was mostly worried about leaving my friends and my school; Carly hated everything about the move (except the horse stables part).

Carly was way better than I was at making our parents' lives pretty much hell for about four months — two on either side of the move.

But through it all, Dad was Mister Rah-Rah ... *you're gonna fall in love with the place, just give it a chance*, I'm thinking, *yeah, right*, and I'm pretty sure Carly was thinking *cut the shit, Dad*.

So, he *can* communicate. But for some reason, this time around, my dad was Mister Nada.

It was two weeks after the funeral that I first heard the words *Manhattan Project*. Of course, I didn't hear them from Dad since we were still in the communication vacuum about what happened at Great-Grandpa Will's funeral. I did find out from reading the paper that the protestors had been released and that "charges were pending depending on what the ongoing police investigation turned up." The *Trimble Times-Herald* said the demonstrators were "… protesting the fact that Mr. Deaver had been one of the architects of the Manhattan Project."

I guess I should have read the rest of the story but I was late for football practice so I didn't. Which meant that the first actual information about the Manhattan Project came a few days later from Lorelei Faber, who, next to Carly and maybe Donald Trump, is my least favourite human being on the planet. If Lorelei Faber was a boy she'd be the school bully. In fact, she'd *be* Donald Trump. But because she's a big, overweight, round-faced, nasally voiced rich kid, Lorelei does her hurting with words, not fists.

Which, come to think of it, *does* make her one of the school's bullies.

Of course, Lorelei being Lorelei, her telling me what "she thought I should know" had a lot more to do with making me feel like crap than passing along useful information.

It was right after school on a Wednesday. Phys. ed. is last class on Wednesdays and since — genius that I am — I forgot my lunch that day, I was dying of starvation and wanting to get home ASAP to tuck into a peanut-butter-and-honey sandwich which might, if I was lucky, save my life.

The good thing is there was no football practice that day. All our coaches are teachers and there was a staff meeting after school, which meant no football. It also meant I could be home and halfway through the peanut-butter-and-honey sandwich in about twelve minutes.

At the top of the stairs as I flew out the doors, still pulling my jacket on — there she was, in all her gory (that's not a typo — it's supposed to say "gory").

"Hey, Larkin," she nasaled at me.

That was another thing about the lovely Lorelei. She called everybody by their last names, even her friends.

I tried to think of something to say that would spare me having to waste more than five seconds of my life on Lorelei Faber … came up with nothing, so I stopped and looked at her.

"Hey, Larkin, did you know your last name rhymes with fartin'?"

"Actually, Lorelei, it doesn't, but somehow I'm not surprised that you don't know that."

She looked at me, and I could tell she was thinking. I could also tell it was a struggle for her.

"At least I don't have anybody in my family who was on the Manhattan Project," she looked around at the gathering crowd of kids who apparently weren't as hungry as I was and had time to stand around and listen to Lorelei Faber put people down.

It didn't look like any of them got what she was talking about any better than I did. I didn't say anything, mostly because I knew I didn't have to. Lorelei wasn't somebody who needed prompting.

"At least none of us —" she waved her arm around to show that everybody was with her on this, which I knew they weren't "— have someone in our family who helped kill millions of people."

If Lorelei was a guy I would have punched her, but there are things you can't do in this life and knocking loud, dumpy girls on their butts, even if they're meaner than snakes, is one of them.

So I opted for silence one more time, hoping that this time she'd be satisfied with the totally lost look on my face and move on.

Fat chance. Pardon the pun.

"You don't even know what I'm talking about, do you, Larkin?"

"Nobody with an IQ of more than seven knows what you're talking about … ever, Lorelei."

"Well, then maybe I'll tell you," she sort of growled it which would have been more effective if it hadn't come out of her mouth all nasal.

"I'm sure you will," I said.

"The Manhattan Project was what they called it when a bunch of scientists got together and built the first atomic bombs, the ones they dropped on Japan and killed thousands of people. That's what I'm talking about, Larkin."

It was a pretty good speech, for Lorelei Faber. And once she said it, it actually made sense. Great-Grandpa Will was a scientist. And there were atomic bombs dropped on two Japanese cities. I knew that much. So if there was something called the Manhattan Project and if my Great-Grandpa had been part of it, that could explain the protestors at his funeral.

I couldn't think of anything to say so I decided my best course of action was to get out of there and get home to the peanut butter and honey.

"Have a nice day, Lorelei," I said and pushed my way through the crowd of kids on the steps. I knew they were all watching me and I also knew that Lorelei and her entourage would be laughing and high-fiving over their "victory." I decided that I wouldn't run or even walk fast, no matter what. But it was hard when I heard Lorelei call, "That's a killer family you got there, Larkin."

Which I have to admit was a pretty good line considering it came from Lorelei Faber. Maybe she wasn't as dumb as I'd always thought. The meaner-than-a-snake part though — I definitely had that part right.

When I got home I had the peanut-butter-and-honey sandwich but it didn't taste nearly as good as I thought it would.

CHAPTER
THREE

Google time.

I wrote a short report from little bits of a bunch of sites that talked about the Manhattan Project. I couldn't believe it. I hated writing reports for school (doesn't everybody?) and here I was writing one for ... what *was* it for? I guess I just wanted to know the truth behind the big "secret".

This was my report ...

> The **Manhattan Project** was a research and development program of the United States, the United Kingdom, and Canada that produced the first atomic bomb during the Second World War. From 1942 to 1946, the project was under the direction of Major-General Leslie Groves of the U.S. Army Corps of Engineers.
>
> Scientists recruited to produce an atom bomb included Robert Oppenheimer (USA), David Bohm (USA), Leo Szilard (Hungary), Eugene Wigner

(Hungary), William Deaver (Canada), Rudolf Peierls (Germany), Otto Frisch (Germany), Niels Bohr (Denmark), Felix Bloch (Switzerland), James Franck (Germany), James Chadwick (Britain), Emilio Segre (Italy), Enrico Fermi (Italy), Klaus Fuchs (Germany), and Edward Teller (Hungary).

The scientists working on the Manhattan Project were developing atom bombs using uranium and plutonium. The first three completed bombs were successfully tested at Alamogordo, New Mexico on July 16, 1945.

On August 6, 1945, a Boeing B29 Superfortress bomber dropped an atom bomb, code named "Little Boy," on Hiroshima, the eleventh-largest city in Japan. It has been estimated that over the years around two hundred thousand people have died as a result of the Hiroshima bomb being dropped. Japan did not surrender immediately and a second bomb was dropped on Nagasaki three days later. The Japanese surrendered on August 10.

After Hiroshima, C.D. Howe, the Canadian cabinet minister assigned to the Manhattan Project said, "It is a distinct pleasure for me to announce that Canadian scientists have played an intimate part, and have been associated in an effective way with this great scientific development."

There were two lines in the whole thing that really stood out for me. The first was the one in the second paragraph that named William Deaver of Canada as one of the scientists who worked on creating the atomic bomb. The second was the one that said two hundred thousand people died that day in August and in the years after the first bomb — the one dropped on Hiroshima. I decided to try to forget words and phrases like "Little Boy" and "distinct pleasure."

My mother's maiden name had been Deaver. So Great-Grandpa Will might have been part of the team that developed the first real "weapon of mass destruction." How did I feel about that?

That was what I had to decide.

For starters how do you get your head around "two hundred thousand people died"? That's not something I'm able to understand. That's about the same number of people as there are in Saskatoon, where we used to live. So, you're going along and one day somebody drops a bomb on your city and kills most of the people who live there. Not all of them die right away — some live and have brutal lives for a while in terrible pain or with horrible sickness.

And then they die.

But there were some who didn't die. The ones who were far enough away from the bomb that they were badly injured and horribly scarred for the rest of their lives, but at least they *had* lives. Two hundred thousand dead.

It's like the Holocaust. All those millions of Jews died and I know it's horrible but I can't get it in my head. I guess that makes me sound like a bad person but I can't help it. You know what I *can* get in my head?

Anne Frank. I read that book a couple of years ago and I felt like crap when I'd finished because I knew she'd died. Her and everyone else in that house except for her father.

I was able to actually feel something because it was one person. Or a few people. And because of the diary, I *knew* them — especially Anne.

I wondered if there were any Anne Frank–type stories about Hiroshima.

August 6, 1945

When Yuko woke up, she was aware of two things.

The first was pain. So much pain. Her head hurt. Not like a headache, more as if her head was on fire. It was like when you burned your hand on the stove, you ran and put it under water. But Yuko couldn't run and put her head under water to cool and soothe it.

Yuko couldn't move. There were things on top of her. Holding her down. Keeping her from moving. Her left leg was hurting terribly. She wondered if it was broken.

The second thing Yuko became aware of was that she couldn't see. She tried to force her eyes open. But then she realized they were already open. And still she could see nothing. Was it because she was in a dark place? Or was there something wrong? Did it have something to do with the terrible pain all over her head?

And suddenly Yuko was afraid. She was more afraid than she had ever been in her life. What was wrong with her? What had happened?

She remembered the flash of light. Did all this have something to do with that flash? Her mother would be able to tell her.

But where was she? Her mother had always been there to help Yuko when she was sick or had the frightening dream — the one about the tall man in the long black coat who was holding on to a great and terrible dog. And in Yuko's dream the man was always saying that Yuko was a horrible child and because she had behaved so badly he had no choice — he would have to release the dog and let it attack her and hurt her.

And Yuko's mother would come into her bedroom and tell her there was no tall man and no dog and that she would always be there when Yuko was sick or hurt or frightened.

Where was Mother now? Why hadn't she come? Yuko hurt so much and she was so afraid. But her mother was not there.

Yuko tried to open her mouth to call her mother but the only sound she made was a hoarse whisper like the old man at the vegetable shop made. And he was very, very old … people said almost one hundred years old. Sometimes you couldn't hear him unless you stood very close, close enough to smell the tobacco and the fresh dirt smell like the old man had been digging with his hands. He always reminded Yuko of the times she and Kiyoshi had gone to their uncle's farm and dug the vegetables for that night's *niku-jaga*, the stew she and her brother loved.

But no one was standing close enough to Yuko to hear the croaking of her whispered cries. Not her mother. Not her brother. No one.

Yuko stopped trying to call out and instead tried to think. Perhaps her mother had gone for the doctor. Yes, that had to be it. She had gone to get Dr. Fujikama. Soon they would both be here to help her and make her feel better.

Yuko did not know that in the seconds after the flash she had seen out the window as she made her way to her brother's room that her mother had died. That her brother had died. And that almost all of their neighbours and the old man at the vegetable shop and all of her classmates from Keiko Hiroshima Prefectural Girls' School and Dr. Fujikama — they had died too.

Yuko did not know that 90 percent of the doctors and nurses in Hiroshima had died in the first minutes after the blast … that only three of the forty-five hospitals remained and that most medicines, dressings and even the most basic medical supplies had been destroyed.

Yuko would not know any of that for several days. For now there was only pain — the searing, burning pain that enveloped her head. If only it would stop.

And then it did. At that moment, the welcome loss of consciousness that would make her forget the hurting, at least for a while — it came then and she fell into a troubled, swirling all-black cloud of sleep.

CHAPTER
FOUR

Carson Tinsley is a deaf kid in my class. He's also my best friend. Carson moved here from Chicago about a month before the school term started. His dad works for Boeing in Seattle and his mom is substitute teaching at the middle school my dad works at.

I met Carson at a football camp in August. He was one of the best players there but because he was new to the area and maybe because of the deaf thing, most of the guys sort of ignored him.

The third day of the camp he forgot his lunch. Carson is large and food is quite important to him. When I saw he didn't have any lunch I sat down next to him and offered him one of my mom's peanut-butter-and-banana sandwiches.

"You sure you got enough?"

I nodded. "Sure, there's lots here. My mom thinks I'm Arnold Schwarzenegger."

"Has she ever looked at you?"

I looked over at him and he started laughing and that was my introduction to the "Carsonian sense of humour" (his term). And the truth is, the guy is pretty funny.

Anyway we were instant friends. The power of food.

By the time school started a few weeks later, we'd spent a lot of time hanging out, throwing the football around, and eating French fries.

I think Carson was the first deaf kid at Weston Comprehensive High School in a really long time, or maybe ever, and it seemed like all the adults at the school — the teachers and principal and everybody — were totally worried about how to deal with it. The first thing we all learned was that you're not supposed to say "deaf." Except Carson used that exact word to describe himself which made the idea of the rest of us walking around tossing out "hearing impaired" all over the place seem kind of stupid.

So the only people in the school who called Carson *hearing impaired* were the adults. All of the teachers had to wear this thing, I guess like some kind of microphone or something and Carson wore a different rig, kind of like headphones, and between the two bits of technology, Carson must have heard enough that he was getting an education.

He was older than us — I figured because of his hearing imperativeness — impairmentivity — whatever — but the cool thing about having a sixteen-year-old in your class when everybody else is fourteen or fifteen is suddenly you have access to a car. And somebody who can drive it.

Which meant that weekends instantly got a lot better.

And because I was the closest thing Carson had to a real friend at our school, it meant I got to ride shotgun in his dad's 2003 Chevy Cavalier on days when Carson got to drive it. A 2003 Chevy Cavalier — not an amazing car and definitely not a big car.

But it was a car.

Carson could read lips and knew sign language too. He could sign as fast as I could talk. I was trying to learn it and Carson was helping me, but I wasn't very good.

The only trouble with the car thing was that when you're driving you're supposed to keep your eyes on the road and your hands on the wheel which meant no reading lips and no signing. So there wasn't a lot of communication with the driver going on in the ol' Cavalier.

That sort of sucked for Carson. He never said anything but I figured it had to bother him. Sometimes when I was talking and laughing with whomever was in the back seat, I'd see him look over and there was a look on his face, I'm not sure what you'd call it but I always felt like crap after that.

On the positive side, being deaf meant he never had to listen to Lorelei Faber. Carson enjoyed pointing that out to the rest of us, especially right after Lorelei had totally destroyed somebody's self-esteem (which is her best thing). Carson would point to his ear and give a big thumbs-up. Yeah, real funny, Carson.

Actually there were two very cool things about having a large sixteen-year-old ninth grader at Weston Comprehensive. Carson not only had a car, he was also one of the biggest freshmen in our school. Which meant he was a very positive addition to the Weston Mustangs football program. Most of the kids on our team were tenth graders (the juniors and seniors had their own team) but Carson and I had both made the team that year. Carson was one of the defensive tackles, I was on special teams — a kick returner — which meant that every game I got my corpuscles crushed by a lot of people the size of Carson.

Some of the kids at school thought that being deaf meant you couldn't speak either. Sometimes Carson was a little difficult to understand, but it wasn't all that tough if you actually made the effort. Maybe that's why Carson and I were friends. I made the effort. Not because I thought it was "the right thing to do" and not even because of the car; I just liked the guy.

Weston isn't a very big school so the ninth and tenth graders play eight-man football. The rules are pretty much the same — there's just not as many people on the field. Weston has sucked for about thirty seasons in a row, but thanks to having a really big, really tough new defensive tackle, we were actually winning a few games that year. Don't get me wrong — we weren't going to the Super Bowl but at least we weren't as bad as a lot of Mustangs teams had been in the past.

Carson wasn't just big because he was older. As I've already mentioned, the guy also really liked food. I mean most teenagers, especially boys, tend to like food a lot. But with Carson, eating was an activity that required as much effort and concentration as rushing an opposing quarterback. And he was good at both.

So two of the things Carson and I did together were eat and talk football. Which is what we were doing during lunch break that day. Both of us had hamburgers in front of us. At least I think that's what they were.

"You want to hear my theory about these burgers?" I asked him.

"Anything to keep my mind off the taste," he said.

"Okay, here it is. These burgers originated on the *Titanic*. When the ship sank, people started grabbing food out of the kitchen knowing they'd be in lifeboats for quite a while. Everybody was throwing food into the lifeboat like crazy. Including a lot of burgers. But somehow they got missed and sat at the bottom of the lifeboat and then in the hold of a rescue ship for several weeks. Somebody, thinking they were pairs of socks, packed them in several suitcases. The owner of the suitcases eventually headed west on a train and settled just outside of Trimble. One of that person's grandchildren became the head cook at our cafeteria and, one day, many years later, came across the burgers in the sock drawer, and, not wanting to waste food, brought them to school and tossed them in the burger warmer thingy.

"And bingo, here they are ... historic burgers sitting on our plates waiting for one of us to suck up the courage to take a bite."

When I'd finished giving my theory on the burgers, a theory which applied to most of the food the cafeteria served, Carson said, "You know, you're weird."

But then he laughed. Carson had this loud laugh that, when you heard it, you couldn't help but laugh, or at least grin, yourself. So everybody around us was grinning or laughing, all because of the horrible burgers, probably the most positive effect the cafeteria had ever had on people.

There was one other thing about Carson ... his wardrobe. He had a thing for red sweaters. Didn't matter if it was winter or summer, indoors or out, Carson would be wearing a red sweater. Apparently it didn't have to be a *nice* sweater — just as long as it was red.

"*I'm* weird?" I looked at him. "You're the guy in the red sweater for day nine hundred and fifty-six in a row."

He nodded and grinned. "Seriously, think about it. You hang out with a deaf kid, you spend all your time reading about some city in Japan, and you don't have a girlfriend."

"That's it? That's all you got?"

"Oh yeah, and you're eating mock-shit hamburger."

I thought about it. And had to admit Carson was right ... on all four counts.

I swallowed a bite, washed it down with orange juice, and nodded. "Okay, let's say you're on to something. I'm going to keep hanging out with you because Lorelei Faber thinks it's a waste of time dropping insults on you, so she stays away and I benefit from that; I'm going to keep reading about what happened when they dropped the bombs on Japan because I'm interested in that; and I'm almost finished the mock-shit hamburger."

He looked at me, eyebrows raised. Waiting.

"So the only thing I can change is the girlfriend thing. And I'm working on that."

"Got anybody in mind?" He cast a quick look around the room.

"Maybe."

"Yeah? Who?"

"Hey, you're my friend, not my therapist. I don't have to tell you everything."

Carson grinned again. "But you will. Eventually."

CHAPTER FIVE

The first meeting of the Weston Comprehensive High School Travel Club took place a few weeks after Great-Grandpa Will's funeral. Things had returned to more or less normal. Lorelei Faber hadn't bugged me much more about the Manhattan Project thing. I figured it was because she had a pretty short attention span.

Don't get me wrong. She and her wing nut pals still bugged me every chance they got, but they had moved on to other topics — my clothes, my hair, how bad my dancing was — the important stuff.

The purpose of the meeting was to do two things — find out how many kids were interested in going on this year's school trip and to pick three or four places as possible destinations. There were twenty-six kids who signed up, although Mr. Pettigrew who was the teacher/advisor for the club said there are usually a few people who sign up but don't actually go.

Lorelei Faber was one of the twenty-six.

With my luck the plane would have to make a forced landing in the jungle and Lorelei and I would be the only ones who weren't injured and we'd have to slash our way through fifteen miles of dense undergrowth to the nearest village to find help. I was looking forward to the trip already.

There were some boring business-y things that had to be discussed; then it was time for the suggestions about where we should go. And after twenty minutes or so we had narrowed it down to France, England, Germany, and Portugal.

That's when I put up my hand.

"Chris," Mr. Pettigrew nodded at me.

"How about Japan?"

He looked at me. "Any reason for that suggestion, Chris?"

"Well ..." I thought about it for a few seconds. "First of all, every suggestion so far has been Europe. I'm just wondering why we couldn't look at other places. I've read some stuff about Japan and it sounds like a beautiful country with a very different culture from ours. Could be a valuable learning experience."

It never hurts to throw out the "valuable learning experience" phrase. Teachers love that stuff.

And guess who helped out. Although not on purpose. Lorelei put up her hand ... and said (and I quote), "That is *so* stupid. Nobody at this school speaks Japanese and I hate sushi."

Mr. Pettigrew said, "Thank you, Lorelei." Although, as I watched him, it looked to me like he was having trouble keeping from laughing.

The thing about Lorelei is that I wasn't the only person at Weston who didn't like her. In fact, Lorelei had done a pretty good job over the years of pissing off a lot of people so whatever Lorelei was in favour of, the large majority of Weston students were opposed to. And if Lorelei was against something you could count on everybody else being in favour. Which meant that Japan made the short list — the three top vote-getters were Japan, Germany, and England.

"I have to caution you," Mr. Pettigrew said, "Japan might be problematic on the financial side — it might just be too expensive."

"See? That's what I was talking about," Lorelei's nasal twang hung in the air.

"Actually you were talking about sushi," Devonne Chelf said.

That got a pretty good laugh. I figured once Lorelei had her gang of female thugs around her (thug-ettes?), Devonne would get a serious mouthful from Lorelei. Which I didn't think would bother Devonne a whole lot. She was about as different from Lorelei as it was possible to get. Devonne was a tall, slender, beautiful African-American girl who was also the star of the Weston Mustangs girls' volleyball team.

"All right, thank you everyone for your suggestions." Mr. Pettigrew stood up. "How about I do some checking into what's available and I'll talk to the school administration as well and report back to you at next week's meeting."

I don't really know why I suggested Japan. First of all, I knew it didn't have much of a shot at being our destination for the very reason Mr. Pettigrew mentioned — money. Japan was a long way away and you heard about people going to Europe all the time. You didn't hear about very many school groups hopping over to Tokyo for a couple of weeks of sightseeing, the theatre, and (yes, Lorelei) the food.

Too far, too expensive, too different.

Too bad.

CHAPTER SIX

I had noticed Julie Lapointe halfway through eighth grade. I kept noticing her pretty much every day after that.

And in the first week back at school this year I asked her out.

Big mistake. I mean she was nice about it and everything, but she told me she was going out with Cody Bamford.

Cody Bamford … who is probably the guy I would most want to be if I couldn't be me. The man is a cliché — quarterback, Brad Pitt looks, smart, and a nice guy. Yeah, that about covers it. If Carson ever lets me drive the Cavalier, I plan to run over Cody Bamford.

Back to Julie. She's kind of tall for a girl, maybe about an inch shorter than me. Long black hair like you see in those commercials, you know the ones where the gorgeous chick turns her head back and forth and her newly shampooed hair flips around in slow motion and looks amazing — yeah, well, that's Julie.

Dark eyes to match the hair and a smile that makes me stop walking. No, I'm serious. A couple of times she's smiled at me in the hall and I've actually stopped walking and just watched her heading down the hall to math or English or something. Luckily, I don't think she's ever noticed me standing as still as a poplar tree and staring at her.

But other people have. At least two people, for sure. One is the very person I'd least want to notice — the always delightful Lorelei Faber. And what Lorelei knows (especially if it's something embarrassing) *everybody* knows. In fact, Lorelei made an announcement about it in the cafeteria. The only good thing about it was that Julie doesn't eat lunch in the cafeteria (probably has an allergy to the hockey pucks disguised as meat loaf), so the effect wasn't what Lorelei had been hoping for. Still, it was bad enough if you happened to be me.

The other person who noticed me noticing Julie was Zaina Nawal. She's in a couple of my classes and she's really smart, but really quiet. Her family runs a Lebanese restaurant downtown. I've eaten there a couple of times — it's great. I think Zaina works there sometimes after school and maybe on weekends.

One of the times I stopped walking after one of Julie's killer smiles, I finally turned back to start down the hall to my next class and almost ran into Zaina. She was also stopped right in front of me. She was also watching Julie. Or maybe she was watching me.

"She is very beautiful," Zaina said.

"What … oh, you mean Julie? Uh, yeah sure, she's okay, I guess." *Nice cover, Chris.*

Zaina smiled. Not a big smile like she was laughing at me, but enough to let me know she had it figured out.

"I wanted to ask you something," she said.

Somehow I figured this wouldn't be a math question. Zaina could math me around the block any day of the week.

"Sure," I said.

"There's a movie at the Variety Theatre on the weekend. It's a Japanese film … English subtitles. I know you're interested in Japan. Would you like to go on Saturday? It starts at seven."

I almost said, "With you?"

Which would have been the dumbest and rudest thing I'd ever said in my life. But for once my brain was working a little faster than my mouth.

Which is why I said, "Hey, that sounds cool. But I'm … uh … not sure I'm going to be around. My dad said something about going to my grandma's for dinner on Saturday. So I don't know for sure but —"

"Sure, that's okay. I understand."

And Zaina Nawal walked away.

I'm pretty sure she saw through the BS I was giving her. Because it *was* BS. My grandma didn't even live in Trimble; she lived in Calgary. How stupid am I?

Thing is I have no idea why I lied to Zaina. Or why I didn't jump all over going to the film with her. First of all, I knew about the movie and was even thinking I'd like to go but didn't really have anybody to go with.

So along comes Zaina wanting to go and she asks me and I sort of blow her off. And I didn't know why. And the other thing about the lie is that it meant I couldn't go to the movie at all now because if she was there, I'd look like an even bigger jerk … damn.

"I need to ask you something," I told Carson while we were sitting in the Cavalier after school, waiting for the Repp twins who were catching a ride home.

"Can't," Carson said.

"Why?"

"I'm not your therapist." Carson grinned at me.

"Shut up," I said.

"Okay, ask me."

I told him about Zaina and how I'd acted like a total loser with her and I couldn't figure out why.

"Maybe you're a closet racist."

"That isn't funny," I told him.

"I'm not trying to be funny. How many girls from other races have you gone out with?"

"That isn't a fair question. I've gone out with three girls in total … and that's only if you count my cousin, which you can't because our mothers arranged that for her birthday and the whole day sucked. So really only two."

Carson shrugged.

"Besides I hang out with you, don't I?" I said.

"Doesn't count. Deaf isn't a race."

"I *like* Zaina. I guess I was just surprised that she asked me out."

"Plus you were drinking in Julie's movie-star beauty right at that moment."

"Drinking in?"

"Uh-huh."

"Yeah, well, maybe. Thing is I feel really crappy about the way I treated Zaina. And if I go back to her now and say *yeah, I'd love to go to the Japanese film at the Variety with you*, she'll probably think I'm feeling sorry for her and hate me even more."

"You know what you need?"

I looked at him.

"A *real* therapist. You're a mess."

I would have argued the point but just then Riley and Jonathon Repp, climbed in the car and the conversation turned to where we should stop for fries on the way home.

CHAPTER
SEVEN

The next day was Tuesday, which meant the second meeting of the Travel Club.

The first thing I noticed was that there weren't as many kids at this meeting. No surprise there — there would always be a few who would come to the first meeting just to check it out, just like Mr. Pettigrew said. Then they'd go home and mention to their parents that "hey we need to fund raise a coupla thou for me to go on a trip with the kids from school" … and that would be the end of it.

Some parents didn't have the money or the will to help fundraise or even give the kid the moral support to make the thing happen.

Those kids weren't at the second meeting of the Travel Club.

Unfortunately, Lorelei Faber wasn't one of those kids. Fabers were big money people — real estate or something — and they could probably afford to send Lorelei on a trip every week. And probably wanted to if her personality at home was anything like at school.

The other thing I noticed which I missed at the first meeting was that Zaina was there. Maybe she wasn't at the first meeting or maybe she was and I didn't see her, I wasn't sure.

I smiled at her and she smiled back and looked like she meant it which made me feel a little better.

The meeting began and the first item of business was to choose an executive for the club. Mr. Pettigrew figured all we needed was a president, vice-president, and secretary-treasurer. There were a few minutes of people looking around the room at everybody else, trying to decide who might do a good job in those positions.

Devonne Chelf was voted in as president, which I thought was an excellent choice. Then Devonne nominated me for vice-president and when no one else was nominated, I got the job. Which I was okay with. For about five minutes.

Then someone with an obviously twisted sense of humour nominated Lorelei for secretary-treasurer. *Just kill me now.*

But then someone else nominated Zaina, which meant an actual election. Zaina and Lorelei left the room during the vote. As they were heading out the door, Lorelei turned and grinned at everybody, her look saying *no way this chick beats the amazing Lorelei Faber for this job.*

As creepy and evil as Lorelei was, she had a fair number of friends in the school. Or at least people who pretended to be her friends. More like followers. I guess there are always going to be people who figure hanging with the bully is better than being bullied.

The vote was close. But Zaina got eleven votes and Lorelei got nine. I almost did the leap in the air and a big "yeah," but I decided a vice-president should act a little more dignified. I stayed in my seat and had a little private inner-celebration.

Lorelei had the same grin on her face when she came back in the room — figuring, no doubt, on a landslide victory. Much as I wanted to, I didn't look at her when Mr. Pettigrew announced the result of the election, but I heard a noise from the area where Lorelei was sitting that sounded like a cross behind a gasp and a word that doesn't get used a lot at the dinner table.

Mr. Pettigrew ignored the noise and welcomed the new executive. "Before I turn the meeting over to our new president, I do have some news," he said. "I made a few calls and there's a program through the Japanese embassy that helps with the costs of school travel to that country.

"There has been a decline in tourism since the earthquake, tsunami, and nuclear accident at Fukushima in March of 2011. As a result, the Japanese government is spending some money to help restore tourism, including school field trips. It looks like we can get in on this funding, which would actually make it a little cheaper to go to Japan than it would to go to the other two destinations on our short list. So that's something you may want to think about as you make your decision."

Devonne strode to the front of the class and asked if there was any discussion on the destination for the trip. Lorelei's hand shot up.

"I did some reading on this whole Japan deal and there's, like, radiation and everything and we could all go over there and get cancer and, like, die."

A couple of kids snickered. Because Lorelei, in addition to being a bully, was also a drama queen.

But Mr. Pettigrew, who was now sitting in one of the student desks raised his hand and Devonne recognized him. Mr. Pettigrew stood up and faced the class.

"Lorelei has a point and it's something we should probably do some more investigating about before making a final decision. How about if your vice-president, who first suggested Japan as a possible destination, and I prepare a report for the next meeting? Are you okay with that, Chris?"

I nodded and Devonne asked for a motion. It was passed that Mr. Pettigrew and I would be a sub-committee to report on the safety of a trip to Japan.

Then we got into a discussion of fundraising ideas and left it that people would bring their ideas to the next meeting.

When the meeting ended Lorelei bolted out the door like her Reeboks were on fire. Loser syndrome. Mr. Pettigrew asked me to stay back for a couple of minutes to decide on a time for us to get together and start researching for our report.

"I hope you didn't mind my volunteering you for this," he said, smiling at me.

I shook my head. "I like this kind of stuff. I'll go on-line tonight and see what I can find out."

He nodded. "Great. How about we meet next Monday at noon in my room and we'll see where we're at?"

"Okay, sure," I said.

As I was leaving Mr. Pettigrew's room, I noticed Zaina a little way down the hall but when she saw me she turned and started walking the other way.

"Zaina," I called.

She stopped and turned back to face me. I tried to guess what she was thinking, but her face was sort of neutral — not mad but not totally friendly, either.

I slow-jogged over to where she was standing.

"Uh … listen … I wanted to say I'm … uh … really sorry about how I acted the other day. I guess I was just sort of surprised that you asked me to the movie and I … was … really … stupid. I mean I even lied about the grand-ma thing and I don't know why. Anyway I really am sorry."

She looked at me for a few seconds and a little smile formed at the corners of her mouth. Which, by the way, was a very nice mouth.

"It's okay, I understand … I guess."

"No, you don't. And you shouldn't … I was a jerk. Thing is I'd really like to go to that film with you if it's not too late. But if you've made other … uh … plans or whatever, I totally get —"

She shook her head. "I was going to go by myself."

"Well, that would be unfortunate," I said. "And unnecessary. Especially when you could have the vice-president of the Travel Club sitting next to you.

VPs are a very big deal, you know. These opportunities don't come along every day." I grinned at her.

"No, I'm sure they don't." Her smile was bigger then and when we'd exchanged phone numbers and headed off in opposite directions down the hall a couple of minutes later I was all \o/.

August 6, 1945

When Yuko woke for the second time the pain was still there … still terrible. But her vision had returned, at least partially. Things were blurry but she could make out objects and shapes around her.

Except there was something wrong. None of the shapes made any sense. She was facing the street in front of her home; she was sure of that. Yes, there … there was the *karatachi* tree that was her mother's favourite. Except it was at an angle now, tipped over so far that the roots were showing on one side. And all of the small orange fruit and white flowers that had been on it yesterday — were gone. The branches were broken and twisted and bare. Still, that was the tree. And this had to be the street Yuko had walked down every almost every day of her life.

But there was nothing left — it was all rubble. The houses were gone. She was confused. It was as if she and her classmates had come along and torn down all the houses. But that was silly.

Besides these houses weren't just taken apart — they were piles of wood chunks, sawdust, and bits of twisted metal, all blackened, like ashes. They were … nothing.

What had happened?

She remembered the flash. It had to be that. The Americans had dropped their bombs. The whispered rumours that had been going on for weeks were true. The air attack they had dreaded but expected had come.

Yuko didn't know that there had been only one bomb. One great and terrible bomb that no one, not even its creators, knew for sure how powerful and incredibly destructive it could be.

It would be some time before the people of Hiroshima realized that what had struck their city that morning was one bomb only. And even then they didn't understand it. How could one weapon do all this?

If only I could move, Yuko thought. But she *could* move. She could turn her head and was able to lift her left arm. Her right arm was underneath her and because she was trapped, and therefore could not move her body, she was unable to do much more than look around and use her one free hand to wipe the water away from her face and eyes.

Except it wasn't water. It was sticky, thick, and warm. It felt like jelly. But how could that be? How could there be jelly all over her head?

And there was still the pain. So much pain. It felt as if someone had pulled all her hair out at once and left her skull open all around it.

She touched her head again. And realized that in a way she was right. She couldn't feel hair. There was no hair. It was all gone and had been replaced by whatever the jelly substance was.

Yuko tried her voice again and this time it worked a little better. She could speak, though not loud enough to yell or even cry out. But she could at least speak.

Not that there was anyone to speak to. There was no one around. No one. She wondered again what had happened to her mother and her brother. But if all the houses in the street had been destroyed, then what about her own house? Maybe that's what happened — maybe her house had been shattered like all the others and she was in what was left of it.

Trapped beneath the rubble.

Panic gripped her like the cold on a winter day. What if no one came to help her? What if there *was* no one to help her?

She would die if she couldn't get out of where she was. She knew that. She would starve or die of thirst or ...

Yuko forced herself not to think of those things. Yet she knew that it was possible that no one would come. She had to try to get herself free.

She tried to twist around to see what was on top of her, what was holding her so cruelly in this unbearable trap. But she couldn't twist.

She tried to move her legs. She was able to wiggle her toes and she could slide one leg back and forth a little and even bend her knee.

One leg and one arm, how could that be enough to get her free of whatever was holding her down? Like a butterfly pinned on a board. She'd seen that once.

Someone … she couldn't think who … had a board like that.

She forced herself to put aside thoughts that could not help her get free. Even forced herself not to think of the unbearable thirst she was feeling, of the need for water. Just a little water.

But then Yuko was aware of something else. A sound. A smell. She strained as hard as she could to move her head in the other direction and finally got her head turned. Looking now not at the street in front of her, but back the other way. Toward the park she had played in so many times. And beyond that the Shinto temple that she loved to visit with her family.

But what she saw was not the park or the temple. What she saw terrified Yuko more than everything that had happened so far.

A wall of flame, a few blocks away perhaps, but surely and steadily moving.

Moving toward her.

CHAPTER EIGHT

Things were going okay. Actually better than okay.

Zaina and I had a great time at the movie — it was a comedy about this married couple who live in Tokyo and pretty much hate each other until one day the wife is travelling in the subway and the train breaks down and she gets out of the train and decides to walk to safety. Of course, she gets lost and the whole time she's down there she's sending texts to her husband and at first they're all *I hate you, you giant bag of squid brains,* and the more lost she gets the more she realizes she still loves the guy and by the end the texts are all, *I love you to death, you lovely bowl of chilled tofu.* Except that the husband only receives the early texts — the squid brains ones.

I know it sounds kind of dumb but it was actually really funny and there were some great scenes of Tokyo (not just in the subway tunnels). It made me want to see Japan even more.

At the end of the evening, Zaina called me a lovely bowl of chilled tofu and we laughed.

"By the way," I said, "I didn't think of it when we made our date the other day ... I mean sort of date ... but anyway, today's my birthday."

Which it was, but the only people who had acknowledged it were my parents, my sister, and Carson. Mom and Dad got me a Russell Wilson jersey ... not bad. My sister gave me a card that she forgot to sign and told me she couldn't believe someone as grotesque as me could have lived this long. And Carson gave me a certificate he'd made up that said I'd get a free chauffeur-driven ride to the destination of my choice if I ever actually had a date.

I didn't bother to tell him that I had a date for later that evening. I decided I'd tell him about it after it happened and if it turned out okay.

"I wish I'd known about your birthday." Zaina smiled. "I could have at least paid for the popcorn or something."

"You *did* pay for the popcorn," I reminded her.

"Oh, that's right. Well, how about this, then?"

And she leaned in and kissed me. Just kind of a peck on the lips. So I kissed her back. Not a peck, but nothing too over the top, either.

I don't know why I did that. I liked her okay, but there was still Julie Lapointe out there just waiting for me to make my move. Yeah, right.

Anyway Zaina didn't seem to mind that I kissed her and I kind of liked it myself. In fact, it was probably the highlight of my fourteenth birthday. Which is saying something because I'm a huge Russell Wilson fan.

The noon meeting with Mr. Pettigrew went pretty well. We'd both done a lot of research and while there was no one-hundred-percent guarantee that we wouldn't encounter some hot spot of radiation, the truth was Hiroshima was pretty safe from radiation (ironic, huh?) because of its distance from Fukoshima.

And it looked like we could definitely get some funding help from the Japanese government that would help a lot.

"We'll have to take it to the school administration and the Parents Council for approval before we can do anything," Mr. Pettigrew told me.

"How tough do you think that will be?"

"Funny you should ask." Mr. Pettigrew grinned at me. "The vice-chair on the Parents Council is Margaret Faber."

I'm pretty sure my mouth dropped open. "As in Lorelei's ...?"

Mr. Pettigrew nodded. "Mom, yeah."

"Crap," I said.

"Well, she's only one vote, so let's not panic just yet. Besides the Travel Club hasn't even decided for sure that Japan's the destination."

"That's true."

"Okay, I've got supervision, Chris. You're welcome to finish your lunch in here. Just close the door when you go out."

"Thanks." I nodded and had my sandwiches spread out in front of me and *Moby Dick* open to page 170 before Mr. Pettigrew was out the door. I had to read fourteen pages for English, Period 6.

I watched as Margaret Faber rose from her chair. If I ever decide to create a piece of art that depicts the term "old bag" it will be as close as I can come to Mrs. Faber getting up out of that chair.

She was Lorelei with thirty additional years and one hundred additional pounds. She had a chest shaped like (and the size of) two Christmas turkeys. As she rose she turned, giving me a look at her never-ending backside. The only thing on her that wasn't big was her face. In fact, it was all wrong for the rest of her. It was sort of … pinched, like a prune with the flu. But maybe that was just because she was mad. Or, as she called it, "indignant."

"I am indignant," Mrs. Faber said and turned in every direction so that no one would miss seeing just how indignant her pinched prune face really was.

"As a parent of a child at this school I want to say how utterly appalled I am that the Travel Club, under the direction of *that man* —" she pointed a stubby index finger with the brightest nail polish I'd ever seen at Mr. Pettigrew — "is wanting to take my child and yours to Japan. Japan —" the second time she said it her voice went up a few notes — "which we all know is the country that attacked Pearl Harbor and started the Second World War. Japan that is now overrun with radiation and is populated with people who … who …" she seemed to be struggling a little at that point, "eat disgusting food and don't even speak English."

Okay, I thought to myself, *Lorelei and her mom had been chatting about the trip.*

Our principal, Ms. Dorel, thanked Mrs. Faber for "her thoughtful insights" and asked Mr. Pettigrew to respond.

He stood up. "I appreciate your concerns, Mrs. Faber, although I should just mention that, in fact, the Second World War was two years old by the time the Japanese attacked Pearl Harbor. As for safety issues, we have done considerable research into the radiation issue. While it's not a foolproof scenario, nothing really ever is when we talk about international travel, I do feel that our students will be safe and will have an enjoyable and valuable experience in Japan. Even though you're right about the fact that the vast majority of Japanese people do speak Japanese."

There were some snickers in the room as Mr. Pettigrew finished speaking. Mrs. Faber wasn't snickering. "Well, I for one will not be allowing my child to go on such an ill-advised trip, I assure you. My daughter is traumatized and terrified at the very thought of going to that place."

"I'm sorry to hear that, Mrs. Faber," Mr. Pettigrew said. "I think Lorelei would benefit from a trip to Japan just as I believe all the students who go will benefit from encountering a culture very different from our own."

Mrs. Faber turned to face the largest group of parents who were behind her. It meant her butt was facing me. It was ... um ... moving. No, I mean it — it was sort of ...

jiggling, which I concluded must be what butts that size do when they're indignant.

Her voice rose another couple of decibels. "I would like a show of hands from all those parents who feel as I do that we simply cannot let this … individual take away our children like some kind of Pied Piper on a trip we absolutely oppose."

That's when the most surprising thing in the history of Weston Comprehensive happened. That's when Lorelei Faber stood up and practically yelled, "But Mom, I want to go to on the trip."

No one said anything for maybe thirty seconds, but several people applauded. Mr. Pettigrew seemed to have suddenly become really interested in the pattern on the ceiling tiles.

And that pretty much brought the meeting to an end. Mrs. Faber huffed and puffed, but you could see her heart wasn't in it. There was a vote of the parents and the trip was approved twenty-four to three.

When it was over, Lorelei was actually smiling, which gave her face a very different look from the smirk that was usually there. And although I wasn't about to head over and high-five her, I had to admit it probably took courage for her to stand up to her mother in public like that. I wondered if I could have done it.

Of course, the downside was there was a pretty good chance Lorelei would be travelling with us to Japan and I wasn't dumb enough to think she was suddenly going to become my BFF. In fact I figured I could count on lots more unpleasant moments on the trip thanks to Lorelei Faber.

Turns out I was right. Except I didn't have to wait that long.

When the meeting was over, a bunch of us were standing around outside talking and joking around some. Lorelei came over to where I was. My mom, dad, Zaina, and I were grouped around a fountain that stood out in front of the school.

I was about to tell Lorelei that I really admired how she'd taken a stand in the meeting. I didn't get the chance.

"Hey, Larkin," she said, loud enough to be heard in downtown Seattle. "Looks like you'll be able to meet up with some of the people that relative of yours blew away."

Like a lot of Lorelei's statements this one made no sense. Which is partly why I didn't have an answer. Nobody did.

Lorelei laughed the laugh of a demented woodpecker and walked off into the night.

August 6, 1945

Yuko tried to scream.

She could tell the flames were moving fast. But as hard as she tried, she couldn't scream. Her voice managed a kind of low mournful moan that only someone very close to her could possibly hear. And there was no one close to her, Yuko was absolutely sure of that now.

She tried to move ... to free herself from the unbearable weight that held her in place and was squeezing her more and more so that even breathing was becoming more difficult. But still only one arm and one leg — and not even her whole leg — were all she could move.

And the flames were coming closer.

That was when Yuko heard something else. It sounded like the pounding of frantic footsteps. *Running* footsteps.

A man came around the massive pile of rubble that lay to Yuko's right. He was running, though not fast. His face was horribly disfigured and it looked as if his shirt had somehow been burned into his skin so that it was difficult to tell what was shirt and what was skin.

He was wearing only one shoe but strangely that shoe looked completely untouched by whatever it was that had happened to this man. It was, it seemed, in perfect condition. The other shoe was gone and the man's bare foot was blackened and blistered.

Yuko tried again to call him and again her voice was not much more than a tired, pathetic croak.

Yet the man stopped. For a moment he looked around as if he were trying to discover the source of the sound.

He had heard her.

Yuko called again. "Please help me, *Oji-san*," she pleaded using the formal word for *sir*.

The man's eyes turned toward her and for a moment, Yuko thought that he had been blinded. His lashes and eyebrows, like his hair, were gone giving his face a strange, expressionless look. He seemed now to be staring at her.

"Please, *Oji-san*, if you could help me …"

The man looked back at her. He stood for a long moment as if deciding whether or not to help. Yuko wondered if because of his injuries the man was dazed and didn't understand.

"I cannot get free," she said. "I am trapped here. If you could please help me …"

Finally the man moved slowly to her and even more slowly began to push and pull rather weakly at the rubble that covered Yuko. She turned her head in the direction of the fire and saw that it was advancing more quickly now and she was directly in its path.

Another man came alongside. She hadn't seen where he had come from. He was wearing only his underpants and was bleeding from bad cuts to his face and shoulder. Still, he helped the first man and they were able to move some of the rubble that covered Yuko.

"You must come out now," the first man said. "And hurry to the river."

Yuko tried and was able to move more than before, but still could not get herself free of the trap that ensnared her.

"We must pull her out," the second man said.

The first man straightened up and said again to Yuko, "You should hurry to the river." Then he turned and limped off leaving Yuko and the second man alone with the fire now louder as it came closer.

There was a smell in the air but only part of it Yuko thought was from the fire. There was also the smell of what might be burned electrical wires. She pushed that thought from her head and tried harder than ever to pull herself free of the rubble.

She knew that if the second man also walked away from her she would die when the fire reached her. The man bent down and strained hard to move one wooden beam that seemed to be holding a lot of the other broken material in place. He was able to move it, centimetres at first, then a little more. He strained at the beam groaning from the effort and the pain of his injuries.

And finally Yuko was able to use both her arms to drag herself out into the open.

The man released the beam and as soon as he did it slid back to where it was. Yuko realized that if she had not been able to get out when she did, she would never have done it.

The man pulled her to her feet. There was still terrible pain in Yuko's left leg and when she looked down she could see an ugly gash running from above her knee down to her ankle. She wondered if she'd be able to walk at all let alone be able to move fast enough to stay ahead of the fire.

"We must go," the man said. "There are many dead people."

Yuko wondered why the man had told her that and once again she thought — as with the first man who had come along — that this man had injuries to his head that made him think and act strangely.

But more than that Yuko knew that this man had saved her life. "Thank you, *Oji-san*, for helping me," she said.

Yuko looked back at what had once been her home. The house, like all the houses for as far as she could see had collapsed completely and was nothing but a pile of wreckage. Yuko knew that if her mother and brother were buried in there she would never find them.

But still she called once.

"Mother ... Kiyoshi."

Though she had tried to call out as loudly as she could, Yuko's voice was still not much more than a whisper. She listened. And heard only the roar of the fire. She could feel the heat now from the flames that were racing toward them. And Yuko turned away from the only home she had ever known and began the flight to ... to what? She didn't know. All she was sure of was that she and the man who had saved her had to go now ... and quickly.

Yuko was able to hobble and hop on her good leg and the two of them moved through the destruction ... away from the fire and in the direction of the Kyo River. It was about two kilometres away and there was a hospital there, Yuko remembered, right at the edge of the river.

They moved slowly at first but the man found a piece of wood and handed it to Yuko who was able to use it like a cane to assist her. She made better time then. They rounded a corner where once Yuko was quite sure a large house with the best vegetable garden in the neighbourhood had stood. It too was unrecognizable and the garden was buried beneath tons of rubble and garbage.

Not all of the houses had been reduced to the small, insignificant piles of pulverized fragments that were everywhere. Yuko stopped and looked at one house to her right. It remained standing, though at a slightly odd angle. Three stories high, the entire front of the house and the roof were gone. It reminded her of the dollhouse her friend Kanna had received a couple of years before from an aunt and uncle who lived on the west coast of Canada.

It felt odd and unthinkably rude to be looking into the rooms of the people who lived in the house. But she could see only one person — a man lying on a bed not moving ... asleep, maybe or ...

Yuko knew that they couldn't be more than a couple of streets from her own house. She tried to remember whose house this was, who lived there. But with so many buildings gone or destroyed it was impossible to make sense of the street and though she thought until her head hurt more than ever, she couldn't say whom the house with no front and no roof belonged to.

The man who was walking beside her stopped suddenly and turned to face her. "I must go back," he said. "My wife is a kindergarten teacher and she left our home and was walking to the school when this happened," he moved an arm around as he said the word *this*. "I have to go back."

"But you can't, *Oji-san*," Yuko said. "The fire is back there. You cannot go back, you must not …"

But he suddenly turned and began walking quickly in the opposite direction, back around the corner and toward the fire. Yuko called out one more time but the man was gone.

She would never see him again.

Her leg was hurting worse than ever, but the heat was more intense and Yuko could see the flames rising high above the debris to the west. She turned and, leaning hard on the makeshift crutch, she began hobbling again … away from the fire and toward the river.

She was forced to weave her way through the piles of rubble that were everywhere and the effort to keep moving somehow was almost worse than being trapped had been. And suddenly Yuko knew she was going to be sick. She turned to her right and her stomach heaved once, then again and for a minute, maybe longer, Yuko was unable to move.

It took all her strength to stay on her feet. She wanted to get down on her hands and knees where it would have been just Yuko and the ground — her being sick into the soft, silent dirt. But there was almost no open ground. Everywhere there were bits of brick and boards, cloth, shredded blankets and clothes, shoes, children's toys, food, garbage, and …

The dead woman's eyes looked up at her. They were wide, frightened eyes, staring up at the sky and the woman's mouth was open, like she had been trying to scream at the moment she died. There was so much blood on the woman she could have been wearing a red dress. Yuko noticed that the blood ended just below the woman's knees, much like a dress would.

A red dress.

Yuko turned from the woman and tried to be sick again but the heaves were dry now. A roar behind her made her turn and look. A giant pile of debris, what had once been peoples' homes or shops had burst into flame. The fire was moving quickly, steadily and for a brief few seconds, Yuko wondered about the fire department. Where were the firefighters?

But she knew they would not come. Though Yuko did not know, *could* not know, what had happened, she was aware that whatever it was, it was bigger than her city, her Hiroshima, could stand up to. She had not seen a policeman or a fireman and now as she hurried again toward the river she saw more dead people and sometimes parts of dead people.

She tried not to think about these people who the day before had lived on the streets near her home; she had seen them in shops and in the park or walking with their families … and now it seemed so many were dead. Burned and dead.

At last Yuko could see the river. And though the pain in her leg and her head were almost more than she could bear, she did her best to go faster.

As she reached the edge of the Kyo River, she stopped and for a moment could only stare. She didn't understand what she was looking at. It didn't make sense. The hospital that had stood so long on the corner near the river was now *in* the river.

Parts of other buildings, vehicles, a wooden ladder, completely intact, books, paper, people's belongings that had once mattered were now just part of a floating mass of flotsam. Meaningless and as lifeless as the people she'd seen lying in the street.

But now there were hundreds of people, many of them in the water to avoid the heat of the fire. Almost all of them were hurt, most badly. There was so much screaming and crying that Yuko wanted to put her hands over her ears to shut out the noise.

A man stopped next to her. His clothes were blood-spattered and he wore the collar of a Catholic priest. One of his arms was hanging, bent and useless. Yet he smiled at her.

"We must go into the water, little flower," he said, "to get us away from the fire."

Yuko looked up at him. "I cannot walk anymore, *sensei*. My legs — I can't …"

The priest reached down with his good arm and lifted her easily. Then he walked into the water until he stood waist deep. They turned and watched the fire and Yuko's breath caught as she realized the devastation was not merely in the streets around her own neighbourhood, but for as far as she could see in any direction.

"I am thirsty, *sensei*," Yuko said. She used the term of respect one used for a teacher or a person in authority. "Please lower me so I can drink from the river."

The priest shook his head.

"Look around you, Little Flower, you see the people who are sick and vomiting?"

Yuko looked and could see in fact that many people were being sick.

"The water is making them ill. We cannot drink it." The priest shook his head again.

"I was sick before, *sensei*, and I had not had any water."

The priest nodded. "There are many people who have been sick since the bombs; that is true. But we must not drink the water, Little Flower."

Yuko wasn't sure how long they stood there in the middle of the river, pushing things away from them as they floated by. And Yuko thought maybe she even slept for a little while against the priest's shoulder. But the pain of her injuries woke her. That and the thirst. She wanted a drink of water so badly.

Finally the priest moved off to the far side of the river. The heat was less now. He called to a man, the biggest man Yuko had ever seen. It sounded like the man's name was Kenji. He came to where the priest was standing, still knee deep in the water.

"Kenji, you know where there is water for drinking."

The huge man, who looked less injured than anyone Yuko had seen so far, nodded. He had a friendly face that was twice the size of the priest's.

"Please bring some for this child." The priest looked at Yuko with an odd smile. "I do not know your name."

"I am Yuko, *sensei*." She tried to smile at him, but she hurt too much and was too weak even for that.

The man-giant did not speak but turned and moved off. Yuko saw at once that she was mistaken about the man being uninjured. As he walked slowly away from them, Yuko could see that his back had been horribly burned, with part of his shirt melted into the red, oozing flesh. Kenji disappeared and was back a few minutes later with a small basin of water.

Yuko nodded thanks to Kenji and gulped the water, spilling some as her hands shook from the pain, and weakness and fear she felt. When Yuko had drunk, the priest said to Kenji. "I have word that the Red Cross hospital is still standing and is partially able to treat people. I want you to carry Yuko there and see to it that she is in the care of a doctor or nurse before you leave her."

Kenji nodded and again said nothing as the priest transferred her to the other man's massive arms.

"You will be fine, Little Flower," the priest said. "I must help others now. You will be in my prayers."

Yuko was barely conscious now but looked at the priest. And somehow she knew that if she lived it would be because of him. She realized too that she did not even know his name. Then as Kenji, who was as gentle as he was huge, started working his way slowly along the river's edge, moving northward, Yuko felt a heavy, cool, dark curtain slide silently and softly over her.

And she lost consciousness.

CHAPTER NINE

Zaina and I had been in the library since right after school. Now it was close to closing time … twenty minutes to nine. Not the school library — we'd gone to the main branch of the Trimble Public Library downtown. I knew that what I was looking for wasn't going to be found in our school library which was okay, but small.

Earlier that day I had told Zaina about GG Will and that he might have been part of the Manhattan Project that had designed and constructed the weapons which had been dropped on Hiroshima and Nagasaki during the Second World War. And I had asked her to help me find out more.

"Why do you want to know?" she had asked me as she leaned on the locker next to mine while I tried to find stuff in what Carson calls "the place where paper goes to die."

Which I had always thought was a little harsh. A lot of the time I am able to find what I'm looking for. This wasn't one of those times.

I had been on my knees pushing textbooks, pulling notebooks, flipping papers, and occasionally swearing. I was searching for a copy of *Elegy Written in a Country Churchyard* that I had photocopied, blown up, and made a ton of notes on for an English assignment that was due tomorrow. If I didn't find it, I knew that I might as well hurl myself from the Seattle Space Needle. A zero on this assignment would just about kill my first-semester English mark — and my average — and leave me grounded for the next couple of decades.

I had a feeling that Zaina found the whole thing a little funny. Yeah, like malaria is funny. I was close to yelling something (not at Zaina — just at the world in general) that I would be sure to regret later except that was when I found the poem — tucked between a French *dictée* and another poem — one I had started to write the first week of the school year. I'd completed exactly one line. I glanced down at it.

Overhead, nothing was speaking …

I quit reading. I figured Thomas Gray who wrote *Elegy Written in a Country Churchyard* was probably turning over in his grave. I rammed my poem back into the dry swamp that was the bottom of my locker, held the elegy aloft like a cheerleader's pom-pom and said, "Aha!"

Zaina smiled and said, "Aha yourself." She didn't seem all that impressed that I had found the missing document and that I would be able to continue seeing her which, of course, would have been impossible if the twenty-year grounding had taken effect.

I hadn't forgotten her earlier question, and as I got to my feet, I said, "Someone in my family might have been partly responsible for the deaths of thousands of people — pretty horrible deaths, by the way. And I want to know as much as I can about it."

That's when I'd asked her if she wanted to come downtown to the library to help me and she'd said sure, which is why we were in the library twenty minutes before closing time.

I'd finished my analysis of *Elegy Written in a Country Churchyard* and had spent the last while looking at books and articles about the bombing of Hiroshima.

I've always liked the smell of libraries. Books and magazines and newspapers have a cool smell, not just the scent of the paper itself. It's almost like the words on the pages are wanting people not just to see the words, but to hear them, feel them, smell them.

I told Carson that once and he said, "I totally get that. The other day when I read that poem you wrote for English I thought right away, *Man, this stinks.*"

Yeah, well that's Carson. But I still think libraries have a great smell. This one did for sure, way better than the funeral home smell. It was a mix of books, floor polish, the flowers on the librarian's desk, and the people, their energy, their curiosity. And there was Zaina, too. I wasn't sure if it was her hair or her clothes or what, but I could always smell fresh strawberries. Just a little, but it was there. Especially when she was close to me like she was now. She smelled good.

We'd found some interesting stuff. There was tons of technical information about all the research that went into building the first bombs and the difference between the bomb that was dropped on Hiroshima and the one that hit Nagasaki. Of course, that wasn't really the interesting stuff.

That came later. Like when we found a series of photographs of the scientists and others who worked on The Manhattan Project. There was one photo of four of the scientists; one of them was William Deaver from Canada. It was hard to tell because GG Will would have been maybe in his thirties when the picture was taken. But even with all the time that had passed I was pretty sure the guy in the photo was my great-grandfather.

I found out some stuff about other Canadian involvement in making the first nuclear weapons. Part of it had to do with the fact that Canada had deposits of uranium which were needed to create the bombs.

And just about the time the PA system was telling us the library would be closing in five minutes, Zaina came across an article that talked about how some of the scientists and technicians who worked on the bomb began to fear what it could do if it was actually used as a weapon.

"Sometimes you read about people who had no choice in doing what they did in the war," Zaina said. "Maybe this is like that."

I think she was trying to make me feel better — trying to make it seem like GG Will wasn't the evil killer those protestors had been yelling about.

I shook my head. "I don't think so. The scientists weren't prisoners. The Manhattan Project was their job. I mean sure, they were doing their jobs, but I think they had a choice."

"Maybe not. I mean you think about a war, maybe it's a case of doing what you have to do to end the war and stop more people from dying."

Actually, I'd read exactly that argument in one of the articles I'd found an hour or so before. In fact, I think that's what the American president — Truman — used to justify dropping the bombs on two Japanese cities. He was saving lives. I wasn't sure I could totally agree with that statement from either the president or Zaina. But since I didn't have a counter-argument, I just shrugged.

"I wish I could talk to GG Will about it," I told her. "I think if he were sitting right where you are and I asked him to tell me about the Manhattan Project, he would. I wish I'd known about it before he died."

Zaina put her hand on top of mine. "Maybe he didn't want you to know. Maybe it was something he wasn't very proud of — something he regretted afterward. Even if it was a job he had to do."

I looked at her. "These were cities, Zaina — with houses and families. I mean I read there were some soldiers there, but mostly it was just people living their lives and …" I stopped and took a deep breath as I looked at her. "I don't know, I mean it wouldn't make everything okay, but I think I'd feel better if I knew he wasn't all *I guess we showed the bastards.*"

"From what you've told me about your great-grandpa, I doubt he was like that."

I nodded slowly. "Maybe."

We didn't have any more time right then because the librarian guy came by and told us the library was closing. The guy had seemed okay before, but now he was a total Grinch.

Apparently at five minutes to nine, if two teenagers are the only people left in the building, this particular librarian goes from, "And what can I do to help you?" to "I want to grind your sniveling little bodies into microscopic particles of waste matter." He pointed to the clock, then at us, then at the door. And with a couple of grunts and a facial expression that screamed *don't ever darken these doors again*, he hustled us out of there like we were carrying the bubonic plague.

I kind of forgot about that because just as we got outside, Zaina's bus was pulling up to the bus stop and she grabbed my hand as we ran for the bus. We made it, but before she got on the bus Zaina got up on her tiptoes and kissed me. I mean we'd sort of done these polite little things before that were "sort of" kisses. This wasn't a "sort of" kiss.

This was a kiss ... with attitude.

CHAPTER
TEN

The next morning I was sitting in the cafeteria drinking coffee — which surprisingly was not bad — waiting for Carson. It was his turn to bring Krispy Kreme Donut Holes — something we did every Thursday morning because our moms both had early meetings. That meant we were at school before almost everybody except the two people who were working in the cafeteria — one was Mrs. Tofu — not her real name, it was Toffel, but you get the idea — and Julie Lapointe.

So actually I was doing two things. I was waiting for Carson and I was watching Julie Lapointe. And feeling a little bit guilty about how much I was enjoying watching Julie. I was having a little internal debate about whether I should be feeling guilty about it

Christian's conscience: I mean there's Zaina, right?

Christian: Well, sort of.

C.C: No, not sort of. You like her, she likes you. End of story. End of ogling Julie.

Christian: I'm not ogling.

C.C: *Definition of ogle — to stare at in an amorous, flirtatious, or lecherous way.*

Christian: Okay, so maybe I'm ogling. But it's not like Zaina and I are boyfriend-girlfriend, right?

C.C: *Bus stop ... kiss ... remember? Friends don't kiss like that, cousins don't kiss like that, your mom and dad — okay, maybe they kissed like that a few years ago ... anyway, my point is —*

Christian: I know what your point is and MY point is I'm going to keep ogl— looking at Julie sometimes.

The argument would have gone on longer, but I heard Carson make one of his Carson entrances into the cafeteria and I turned my attention away from Julie and watched/listened to Carson head for the serving area to get some coffee. He turned and gave me the drinking sign to ask if I wanted another cup. I shook my head. And watched as he poured himself a coffee, and ladled three spoons of sugar into the cup.

Today's red sweater was beyond ugly. And it had a decorated Christmas tree on the front. Since Christmas was still more than two months off, it made no sense. But most of Carson's sweaters made no sense.

There was one thing that was bothering me. Something more important than today's sweater choice. And it was bothering me a lot.

I'd been trying to talk Carson into joining the Travel Club and coming on the trip to Japan. He'd been saying no, that he didn't have any interest in travelling several thousand kilometres so he could sit with the same people he sat with in the lunch room every day.

I wasn't sure I believed him. I guess what was bothering me most was the thought that maybe Carson wasn't coming because he thought the school's deaf kid wasn't welcome on the trip. That there were people who wouldn't want him there.

I even asked him about it. But he was all jokes and smart-assing like he always is. "Yeah, like I want to spend more time with you and Lorelei Faber. Actually, Lorelei would be okay — it's you I need a couple of weeks away from."

We laughed and punched each other on the arm, but I still didn't believe him. Sometimes with Carson, you had to look past the one-liners to see what was really going on inside his red-sweatered self.

There was something about the way he looked at me whenever the Japan trip came up that made me think that there was a big part of my best friend that wanted to go. So why wasn't he? I knew it wasn't the money. His parents would have put up the money in a heartbeat.

So what then? I guess I'd already answered my own question and I hated the answer. I wasn't kidding myself. Like any kid who's even slightly different from every other kid at school, Carson had taken his share of the bullying. Even had a fight with the biggest bully-jerk in the school — Bill Kohut, who was sort of Lorelei Faber without braces and bra.

Kohut won the fight, but it hadn't been easy and after that most kids left Carson alone. Most but not all.

Not Lorelei, for example. I wondered if it was Lorelei that was keeping Carson from signing up for the trip. Then I realized that couldn't be it. Unlike me, Carson would not be intimidated by the school bully-ette. I finally decided that what was keeping Carson from coming to Japan with us wasn't what the other kids thought of him — it was what *he* thought of him. And if I was right, that was totally sad.

A couple of weeks after Carson's fight with Kohut, I happened to head into the school library and there was Carson, sitting back in one corner reading one of those giant pictorial books … about Japan.

I thought about racing up to him and saying something brilliant like, "So you *do* want to go to Japan. Let's go get you signed up."

But for once I kept my mouth shut and eased my way out of the library without him seeing me.

But since that day I'd been wondering … and worrying … about my friend. And I was still worried as I watched him, coffee in his left hand, Krispy Kreme bag in his right, amble over to where I was sitting.

He sprawled in the chair across from me. I reached for the bag of donuts but he held them away from me.

"Uh-uh-uh, what're the magic words?"

"I didn't have breakfast and if I don't have a doughnut hole in the next fifteen seconds I will probably die."

"Well, not exactly word for word, but close enough."

He set the bag between us and for the next few minutes we downed donuts and drank coffee, two guys just climbing the Stairway to Heaven.

When we came up for air, he looked over at me. "How was the date with Zaina?"

"How did you know about Zaina and me?" I hadn't told Carson, or anybody else, that Zaina and I were going downtown last night.

"I saw you two heading for the bus stop after school. A mid-week date … must be serious. So, how did it go?"

"A) it wasn't a date, and b) it was fine."

"So what was it — a movie? Something a little more cultured — a play, maybe? Something from the sporting side — ice skating —"

"The library."

He paused mid bit-bite. "I'm sorry," he shook his head, then banged his temple with the palm of his hand. "For a second there I thought you said you took your girl to the library."

"Ha, ha. We were working."

"Of course you were," he said, then laughed the laugh that made me laugh even when I was pissed at him.

"Let me ask you something," I said.

"Is this a relationship question? Because if it is, I'll need another donut before I answer."

"And if it isn't a relationship question?"

"I'll still need another donut before I answer."

I told him about the research I'd been doing into GG Will's life and the conversation Zaina and I had had about my great-grandfather's role in the Manhattan Project.

Carson turned serious, as I knew he would. One of the cool things about the guy was that he knew when kidding around ended and real talk started.

He pushed the donut bag to the side and leaned toward me, his elbows on the table. But he didn't say anything right away.

"That's a tough one, Chris," he said. "People have things that they did a long time ago — sometimes it was really great things like war heroes and stuff, but they don't want to talk about it. And sometimes it's not so great stuff and they don't want to talk about it because it makes them feel lousy."

I nodded. "Thing is I don't know which this is. I mean it's hard to see making the world's first nuclear weapons as something heroic."

He shook his head. "I'll bet there are a lot of people who would disagree with you. I mean if there hadn't been a Manhattan Project and the war went on for a few more years, maybe even more people would have died."

President Truman again.

"Or what if the other side got atomic weapons first?" he added. "You think they would have hesitated to use them?"

"Yeah … I guess maybe you're right."

"So what do you want? You want to know that your great-grandfather wasn't part of the Manhattan Project?"

I started to shake my head but it turned into a nod. "No, that's not it."

"Then what is it?"

"I guess I don't want to be ashamed of my GG Will."

"And who says you should be?"

"Those protestors, for starters."

"Protestors aren't always right." Carson pointed at my copy of *To Kill a Mockingbird* that was sitting on top of my binder. "There have been places that banned that book. And there were protests. Which is crazy. So does that mean whats-her-name shouldn't have written it?"

"Harper Lee," I said. "No, it doesn't mean that."

"Exactly and —"

He stopped because just then Lorelei Faber and her entourage crashed into the cafeteria. And even though Carson couldn't hear them, he saw me look at the doors, and turned to see what I was watching.

He turned back to me. "Let me ask you something … is this about your great-grandpa or is this about you?"

For a second I wanted to be mad — real mad. But then I realized I'd asked myself the exact same question. I nodded.

"You're right — part of it is about me. I can't help it. I really liked having this cool guy in the family that I was proud of. And now I don't know if I should be proud of him anymore."

"Okay, you asked me what I think, this is what I think." He stood up, gathered up his books, and looked down at me. "I don't think you should give up on your great-grandpa just yet."

I don't know if he was planning to say more than that because there was a lot of banging chairs and crashing and yelling and I looked over at Lorelei and her gang again. And just like before, Carson looked back at them too. "Shit, I'm outa here. I'll see you at football practice."

And he was gone. I grabbed the donuts and my books and made for the doors. But I wasn't fast enough, I was through the doors and partway down the hall but I still heard Lorelei's very loud, very nasal voice.

"Hey, check it out. It's the baby killer's great-grandbaby!"

CHAPTER ELEVEN

Football practice that day was a little intense. The season was winding down and we had our final game coming up on the weekend against our hated rivals — the Central Raiders.

We'd done okay this season: three wins and four losses, which amounted to a huge year by Weston football standards. But this was Central, and they hadn't lost a single game in four seasons.

Central had black uniforms, a bad attitude, and some seriously badass players. Most of them were big enough to bench press large farm animals. They had won the state eight-man football championship nine times in the last eleven years. And they hated us as much as we hated them.

The thing about a rivalry, though, is it's a lot more interesting if both teams involved in the rivalry win some of the games. We hadn't beaten the Raiders in maybe a half century. The guys who were on our team the last time we beat Central wore leather helmets and travelled to away games on horse-drawn wagons. Okay, maybe I'm exaggerating a little, but the point is — it's been a very long losing streak for the Mustangs.

And just to add a little pressure, Carson, yes, *that* Carson, stood up in the locker room at the start of the practice and announced to the team that he was guaranteeing a win against the Raiders.

Which was stupid. We'd played them in our second game of the season and they'd squeaked out a 54–7 win. A better guarantee would have been that we would all survive the game. There was at least a 50-50 chance that might happen. Us beating them? Not so much.

And now here we were just three days away from our second meeting with the dreaded Raiders and like I said, things were a little … intense.

The coaches were yelling a little louder than usual, everybody was hitting the sled a little harder, and there was almost no kidding around, which is normally a big part of practice.

Carson, in addition to making rash predictions (make that *guarantees)*, was one of the few guys on our team who was as big as the guys who play for the Raiders. Which might have something to do with his rash promise. He might have wanted to look around the dressing room at his teammates before opening his mouth.

I think I mentioned I was a kick returner — punts and kickoffs. I was also our backup running back. I didn't play much running back in games, which was okay when the opposition was the Central Raiders. I planned to spend most of my time on the sidelines praying that our regular running back, Jayron Fitch, did not get hurt.

And to round out my resumé, I was also the back-up place kicker, but that doesn't really count since place kickers never get hurt. I'd only actually kicked a few times in practice and I pretty much sucked at it. I think the only reason I got the backup job was that nobody else wanted it.

I don't know if it was Carson's guarantee or not, but Coach Siggs (he was *Mr.* Siggs in science class) seemed a lot more ... uh ... tense than usual. And when I dropped two punts in a row, I was quickly aware that there are times that not being able to hear isn't the worst thing in the world.

Then disaster struck halfway through the practice. I immediately blamed what happened on Carson. That whole guarantee thing? Bad karma. How else do you explain that on an absolutely harmless play, our biggest offensive lineman, a kid named Desmond Washington (yes, his nickname is Denzel) broke his clavicle (that's his collarbone to you laymen). Jayron Fitch fumbled a handoff from Cody Bamford and normally that would just end the play. But Denzel — maybe trying to light-en the mood — dived for the loose ball. Then about five of us piled in there after it and suddenly there was this yell and Denzel was rolling around on the ground like he'd been shot.

And, uh-huh, clavicle reconstruction — out eight to ten weeks. Kind of a bad deal when the game against Central was four days away.

So from that point on Carson was having to play both offense and defence, which was okay in practice, maybe, but in a game — *this* game — the guy would be dead by halftime.

I was still amazed that a deaf guy could do what he did on the football field. During games Carson wore this hearing aid that was designed especially for Derrick Coleman. He plays for the Seahawks and is the only hearing-impaired player in the NFL. The only trouble was now Carson would have to work his magic on both sides of the ball. Not easy.

Did I mention bad karma?

I guess that's why Coach Siggs gathered all of us at the end of practice to take a knee in a circle around him while he spent fifteen minutes explaining to us (at a high-decibel level) that we had a choice to make. We could be men or we could be cowards. It was up to us. Did we care about our school? (We all yelled yes!!) Did we care about our teammates? (Yes, again!!) Did we care about ourselves? (I think we were supposed to yell even louder there, but I think some of us remembered that we'd be without Denzel and we kind of blew the response — it sounded like a cross between a groan and a hiss.) The coach looked let down and he stared at us for quite a long time, then said, "Okay, twice around the field and hit the showers."

I have to admit, the coach's speech was pretty effective. I'm pretty sure that was the fastest the twenty-two guys on our team had ever run around the football field. Would have been twenty-three but … well, the bad karma thing. But even so, we ran our heinies off. Now if we could just figure out a way to play the game so that all we had to do was run around and never get hit by any of the Cyclops that played for the Central Raiders, this game would be in the bag.

The next day I met up with Carson after social studies when we both had a spare (well, actually it was "study hall," but today it felt like a spare). We wandered out to the Pitt Stop, which is the common area in the school but it's called the Pitt Stop because a few years before, an eleventh-grade kid named Randy Pitt was killed when a lady lost control of her car and hit Randy on the sidewalk right in front of the school. It was a few years before I came to Weston, but everybody knows the story — how the lady managed to miss a bunch of other kids that were close by and ran into a tree instead and was badly injured. Anyway, that year at Grad, it was announced that the common area would be known as the Pitt Stop from that time on. Which I always thought was one of the cool things about our school.

In a dazzling display of reckless courage, I bought a hot chocolate from a machine that looked harmless but obviously hated human intestines. I had learned that sad truth earlier in the year. Carson, who's kind of a sugar junkie, grabbed a soda and we sat down at a table near the windows so we could a) see what we were drinking and b) dream about the freedom that existed on the other side of those windows.

"A couple of things I'd like to discuss," I said, after a sip of almost-drinkable hot chocolate.

"What is that?" Carson pointed at the cardboard cup I was holding.

"Motor oil and rat puke; it's really good."

"Looks like it." He grinned. "So, what are we discussing?"

"First of all — what were you thinking with your guarantee that we would beat Central? Are you completely nuts?"

"We're gonna win," he said.

"Okay, that answers my question. You *are* completely nuts."

"And your second point?"

"Why aren't you coming to Japan?"

"I already told you." He swigged soda.

"What you told me doesn't make sense."

He set his drink down and leaned on the table to look closely at me. "Chris, I don't want to go to Japan, okay?"

"Would you go if we'd picked a different place?" I had a sick feeling that my holding out for Japan had taken my best friend out of the trip.

He hesitated, then shook his head. "No."

"Seriously?"

"Seriously."

"Because I'd feel like a jerk if you'd always wanted to go to Germany or England and I'd ruined that."

"If I'd wanted to go to Germany or England, I'd have joined the Travel Club and come to the meetings. Travel's not my thing."

Hearing him say that made me feel at least a little better. I sat back on my chair and took another sip of swill.

"Okay," Carson said, "I got one for you."

I nodded. "Go."

"Why do you want to go to Japan?"

"Cool country, amazing technology, wonderful culture, Mount Fuji, sushi ... what more could a person want in a country?"

Carson nodded. "Right."

We sat for a while before he spoke again. "Are you sure, Chris? Are you sure this isn't about your great-grandfather being part of the bombs that were dropped on Japan. Is this like the ultimate guilt trip?"

"Oh, good one. Guilt *trip*. Very clever." I started to shake my head but didn't get very far. "You want the truth?"

"Always, bro."

"I have this weird idea that I can go over there and do something, you know, something that would somehow make up for what GG Will did."

"And you call me nuts." He said it softly.

I nodded. "I know it's crazy, but I can't help it. I keep having these thoughts that maybe there's something I can do to ... I don't know ... make a difference. Like I said, it's crazy —"

Carson reached over and grabbed my arm. "It's not crazy, Chris. What it is ... is unnecessary."

I stared at him over the top of my cup. "Unnecessary."

"Yeah. There's nothing you can do that's going to change what happened seventy years ago. Or make things better. And you don't have to. You're not to blame."

I thought about what he'd said. Sometimes having a friend who's a couple of years older is like having a big brother. This felt like one of those times.

"Maybe I'm not to blame. But my great-grandfather, he —"

"Maybe he's not to blame, either."

"What do you mean?"

"Maybe he was doing what he had to do."

"That's kind of what Zaina said."

"Smart girl."

"Do you really think that's what it was — my GG Will just doing what he had to do?"

"It was war, Chris. People follow orders in war. They don't have a choice."

I wondered about that last part but I also appreciated what my friend was trying to do. "Zaina's not the only smart one. You're pretty bright yourself."

He looked at me kind of funny. "What brought that on?"

"For a deaf kid you're not that dumb."

He grinned. "*Deaf and dumb*. Not bad. Not as good as *guilt trip*, but not bad."

We were both laughing. "I'm starting to think I might be your friend even if you didn't have a car."

"And I'm starting to think I might be your friend even if your mom doesn't make great meat loaf."

We both laughed again but I stopped when I looked into my cup and realized I still had to finish the last half of my drink.

CHAPTER TWELVE

Even the Central Raiders uniforms were scary. The crest on their jerseys was a pirate, but this pirate wasn't Jack Sparrow or Long John Silver. This dude looked mean enough to murder your family and eat your pets.

And the worst part was the pirate on the crest was the nicest thing about the Raiders. Things turned really ugly after that. The guys actually wearing the jerseys with the pirate on the crest made you think pirate-guy was a sweetheart.

One thing the Raiders did that seemed to work really well for them was their entrance onto the field. They came out running as fast as they could and screaming this bloodcurdling screech … shriek … something that no one (except maybe other Raiders) could understand, but sounded like the perfect accompaniment for pet-eating.

During the toss of the coin to decide who would kick and who would receive, their captains would glare at opposing captains like werewolves patrolling the streets for a late-night snack. I talked to some guys on other teams and they wouldn't even try to look at the coin when it landed. They'd just go with whatever the Raiders captains said, which generally went something like, "Well, lookit that, it's heads, we win another toss — guess we'll receive."

Yeah, the Raiders were pretty good at the intimidation thing which is maybe why we were down 14–0 at the end of the first quarter. And it would have been worse except for the fact that the Raiders were the most penalized team in the league (now there's a surprise) and had a few major plays — including a long touchdown pass — called back.

Early in the second quarter the Raiders were up to their old tricks and had a pretty good drive down the field brought to an abrupt halt by a personal foul — which is code for "dirty play." That was their fifth personal foul and we were only seventeen minutes into the game.

This latest infraction involved a Raiders player trying to remove one of our linebacker's heads by twisting it around 360 degrees. Twice. So the Raiders were kicking which meant I would be returning a punt against a bunch of very large people, all of whom were in a really bad mood.

I caught the ball, looked up, and saw two Raiders — who, I'm pretty sure were from the original cast of *Texas Chainsaw Massacre* — bearing down on me. I quickly decided that my survival depended on getting out of bounds before Leatherface and his brother got to me and was making my way in that direction when suddenly Carson cut in front of me and mowed both of those guys down like pins at the Holiday Bowling Palace.

The result was there was suddenly a lot of space in front of me and I raced forward, the whole time waiting to be mashed like rocks in a gravel crusher. But I kept running and was at midfield when I realized that no one had laid a hand on me and that there wasn't a Raiders jersey in sight.

I turned on the jets. I'm pretty fast when I'm either scared or I think I might score the first touchdown of my football career. When you put the two together I'm a regular Usain Bolt.

I crossed the goal line untouched. Huge celebration on the sidelines. I was dancin' partly because I'd scored, but mostly because I was still alive.

A couple of minutes after my touchdown, the Raiders did something they almost never do. Their running back — a kid named Rodriguez who was leading the league in touchdowns and yards rushing — fumbled. One of our d backs picked up the loose ball and ran it in for the touchdown. The impossible had happened. We were tied at halftime.

Our locker room was this weird mix of *what the hell happened out there* and *wow, we can beat these guys*. I personally was having a little trouble with that second idea. You had to think that their coach was over in the other locker room telling them to lay off the penalties and get out there and destroy those pantywaists from Weston.

Apparently the Raiders' players didn't get the memo on the penalty thing because on their first set of downs in the second half, they had a long touchdown run called back. Then the first time we got the ball, Cody Bamford threw a pass to Jayron Fitch that went seventy-eight yards for the touchdown.

And it went like that the whole second half — back and forth, they'd score then we'd score and it came down to the last minute of the game and we were only losing by six points, 40–34. Which I considered a major moral victory. Even if we wouldn't be able to make good on Carson's guarantee.

All Central had to do was take a knee a couple of times and the game would be over. But apparently the Central coach wasn't happy that the Weston weenies had kept the game this close. So they came out with a running play — which, meant, of course, giving the ball to Rodriguez and letting him work his magic which had already resulted in three Central touchdowns. Except that somehow Rodriguez ran into one of his own guys and for the second time that day fumbled the ball.

And Carson Tinsley, who had played almost every play in the game and was so tired he could barely stand up, picked up the ball and lumbered (that's what sportscasters call it when a really big guy runs) into the end zone.

The game was tied with no time on the clock. If we could kick the point after, we would beat the Central Raiders for the first time since the invention of running water.

We lined up for the point after. J.T. Kendrick was our kicker and he was pretty good — he made most of his field-goal tries and never missed a convert. But he missed this one. In fact, he never got the kickoff. One of the Raider guys came blazing in from the outside and drilled J.T. before he could kick the ball.

That's when things got … um … interesting. J.T. didn't get up and when he finally did, you could tell he didn't even know what town he was in. The other thing that happened was that the guy who hit J.T. was offside by a couple of yards, which is why he was able to get to J.T.

That meant we'd have to kick it again. With the substitute place kicker.

Me.

When Coach Siggs realized J.T. was hurt he wasn't even sure who the substitute kicker was. And I wasn't about to remind him. At that moment I would rather have kissed Lorelei Faber on the lips than go out on that field and try for the extra point. And, for a second, it looked like I wouldn't have to. Coach Siggs yelled for the offence to go back on the field and go for the two-point conversion. But just as I was thinking *wise decision, Coach* … he changed his mind and yelled the three words I least wanted to hear.

"Place-kicking team!"

I thought about faking an injury, but seeing as I'd been jumping around celebrating Carson's touchdown a few seconds before, I knew that wouldn't work. I thought about pretending I was having a heart attack, but I wasn't sure what the symptoms were.

And before I could come up with a better idea, Carson had his arm around my shoulders and we were heading out onto the field.

"You can do this, buddy. Just relax."

I moved my lips to try to answer, but no sound came out of my mouth.

We lined up for the kick. I didn't even try a couple of practice kicks because I didn't want anybody to see how bad I was.

Cody was our holder and he knelt down to take the snap. He looked at me, nodded once, then yelled "hut-hut." The snap came back to Cody, he set the ball down, spun the laces away from me, and it was up to me. I hesitated.

Finally realizing the ball wasn't going to go anywhere unless I actually kicked it, I stepped forward and gave it my best shot. *Keep your head down, eye on the ball, and follow through.* I knew that's what I was supposed to do and I that's what I tried to do. But I'd waited too long. The ball hit one of the Raiders players. I turned away, disgusted with myself.

Which meant that I missed seeing how the ball had glanced off his shoulder, gone up in the air, bounced on the crossbar, and fallen over the bar with all the slow-motion grace of a drunken duck. (That's not my phrase, by the way. That's how the *Trimble Times-Herald* wrote it up the next week in the paper. Front page.)

The first I knew that we had won the game was when our guys were pounding me on the shoulder pads and screaming and yelling, "We did it, we did it!" So I screamed and yelled, too, even though it wasn't until the next day when I saw the team video of the game that I actually found out what had happened.

All our fans raced out on the field and it was pretty much mayhem. The teachers, parents, students, everybody was hollering and hugging and high-fiving. The best hug came from Zaina, Jeez, I'd survived the Central Raiders and my girlfriend almost broke my ribs after the game. Oh, yeah and she kissed me, too. The whole thing was amazing. Until, OMG, Lorelei Faber, grinning and whooping, mussed my hair. She *mussed my hair*.

I should have faked the heart attack.

And that was it. Except, of course, for Carson reminding us every day for the next month that *he had guaranteed the win*.

CHAPTER
THIRTEEN

The noise was unbelievable. You'd have thought we were a bunch of eight-year-olds running outside for recess.

The bus driver was shaking his head. *You should be glad all you have to do is drive us to the airport, buddy.*

I was trying to play it cool but the truth is I was just as excited as everybody else. In about sixteen hours we'd be landing in Tokyo. Who wouldn't be stoked about that?

It had been a month since our big win over the Central Raiders and the time had flown by as everybody got ready for the trip. Winter had arrived early, which was great because that helped with my part of the fundraising for the trip. I shovelled what seemed like a bajillion (but was probably more like thirty or forty) sidewalks, driveways, and even the United-Methodist Church parking lot ... twice. The result was $728 in the trip fund and for a few days I was my dad's hero.

And even though Dad had said all the money I raised would go to help pay for the expenses, Mom made sure

I got some of it for spending money. She'd converted about $500 to Japanese yen and given it to me that morning at the school as we loaded our gear into the storage area underneath the bus.

Everywhere I looked parents were giving kids last-minute instructions. Mine were doing the same thing. *Stay with the group. Don't spend all your money in the first few days. Listen to the teachers and the parent supervisors. Wash your hands lots. Be polite.*

Even Carly was there, although I noticed she'd had trouble tearing herself away from texting long enough to manage a quick wave that looked more like shooing away a fly. I suspected she might be having a little inward celebration now that her evil brother was going to be far away for a while. Yeah, very few Carly-tears were shed that morning.

Principal Dorel made a speech in the parking lot and I think it was pretty good — her speeches usually are — but I couldn't hear a lot of it because of the general hum of noise from twenty-three excited fourteen- and fifteen-year-olds. I heard the ending though when she hollered "Bon voyage and God speed!" Everybody cheered.

Finally we started climbing aboard the bus. Zaina and I had already agreed we'd sit together on the bus *and* on the plane. We had been learning Japanese online for the past month and she was getting pretty good at it — much better than me, maybe because she had already learned one second language and picking up another wasn't that hard for her.

I grabbed a seat on the right-hand side of the bus and looked out at all the parents. Some were already moving off toward their cars. Others, like mine, had apparently decided to stay until the bus actually pulled away. The three parent supervisors, who were going along to help Mr. Pettigrew, all sat near the back of the bus.

Zaina was still outside with her parents, saying her final goodbyes, I guess. I watched her for a couple of minutes. I was still pretty much amazed that I actually had a girlfriend, sort of. We'd both agreed that we weren't going to get stupid-serious (Zaina's term), but that we'd only go out with each other and that we'd hang out together at school and stuff. And though I didn't tell Zaina, I'd even made an internal promise not to ogle Julie Lapointe anymore. Which, if you ask me, is getting pretty close to stupid-serious.

There was last-minute stuff — parents running up to the bus with something their kid had forgotten, two sisters, Jocelyn and Jolene Plouffe, arriving just as the bus driver announced that he couldn't wait any longer and we'd have to leave without them. And selfies. A lot of selfies. Kids with their parents, kids with other kids, kids with their pets, kids with the bus driver … yeah, a lot of selfies.

There was more but I lost track … and interest.

I let my gaze wander over the crowd of adults outside the bus. That's when I noticed Carson roaring up in front of the school and pulling up to the curb behind some of the parents cars. He jumped out of the Cavalier, climbed up on the hood, and waved at the bus like a madman or someone who'd had way too much coffee.

Except I knew he wasn't waving at the bus or even the people on the bus. He was waving at *me*. I managed to get the window open, and most of the top half of my body out through it. I waved both arms until I thought they'd fall off.

And even with all the noise, which had started to die down a little, I could hear him yell, "Eat some sushi for me!'

I waved one last time, pulled myself back into the bus, and sat in my seat, grinning. Not only did I have a girl-friend — I had maybe the coolest best friend on the planet. That's when Zaina slid into the seat beside me. She looked as happy as I was. She leaned over and kissed me on the cheek, then took a couple of selfies — her and me with the school in the background through the bus window.

I gave my parents one last wave. My dad's lips were moving — I guessed he was mouthing one last instruc-tion: *Don't forget to change your underwear* or something equally dumb. Mom was wiping a tear or two. Moms do that. Some dads, too, but not mine.

As the bus finally started moving, I sat back and looked over at Zaina and smiled. Up until this very minute I kept thinking something would happen and the trip would somehow be cancelled. Like I'd get yellow fever or some other weird sickness and wouldn't be allowed out of my house, let alone out of the country; or there'd be an air-line pilot strike or Dad would be transferred to a private school in Buffalo, New York, and we'd have to move.

But none of those things had happened, and with a final honk of the horn, our bus eased out onto the street and we were on our way. Next stop — Seattle-Tacoma International Airport. And after that ...

We'd be on our way to Japan.

August 6, 1945

Yuko remained in the Red Cross Hospital for nine weeks. But her condition did not seem to be improving. Her scalp, so badly burned and scarred, did not get better. Pus still ran from the worst of the sores on her head. And the pain was almost unbearable.

But the Red Cross nurses and doctors, who seemed never to sleep, were always nice to her and did their best to make her as comfortable as they could. Almost every day, the people in Yuko's hospital room changed. She knew some died, though no one ever said that to her. Others were moved to other parts of the hospital or even to other hospitals in other cities. Still others became well enough to leave and return to their homes — if they still existed — or to makeshift shelters constructed by the occupying forces who were now in control of Japan.

Doctors had operated on Yuko's leg twice. But though it hurt less now, it didn't seem to Yuko that her leg was right. She thought, though she couldn't be sure without standing up, that it was shorter than the other.

On October 12, Yuko was taken in a transport truck to the Catholic General Hospital in Tokyo. She would stay there for another two months. Though the worst of the sores and scars on her head had healed as much as they would, her hair had grown back only in bits here or there. She would wear a head scarf every day for the rest of her life.

Her injured leg had healed, but Yuko had been right: it was more than an inch shorter than the other. She would always have a limp. And she would always be aware, with every step she took, that people were looking at her. The girl with the scars and the limp.

None of her family had survived the blast and though she returned to Hiroshima almost a year after the bomb, she saw only a couple of her friends and only a handful of the people she had known before that hot August day almost a year before.

Though Yuko had always planned on going off to university one day, she now was happy to get work tending the grounds and gardens of two government buildings, and taking classes in the evenings. Seventeen years after the bomb blast, she married and would eventually have two children, one boy who did not live to see his first birthday, and one girl.

Her daughter realized the same thing most of the people who knew Yuko were aware of. Though she never complained and, unlike many of the Hiroshima survivors, didn't rail on and on against the Americans who had dropped the bomb ... Yuko seldom smiled.

And she never ever laughed.

PART 2

THE JOURNEY

CHAPTER
FOURTEEN

Tokyo is huge. Take a city the size of Trimble with its seventy thousand people. Then just add eleven million more people and you've got Tokyo.

Amazement. And maybe a little fear. That pretty much describes what I was feeling — what all of us were feeling — when we arrived at the Narita International Airport. The terminal was bigger than our schoolyard and people were everywhere speaking maybe a dozen languages, none of them English. With all the noise, the flashing lights and signs, and so many people — all of them in a hurry, those first minutes in Japan were stressful.

Mr. Pettigrew had told us we would be met at the hotel by our guide. That meant we had to get *to* the hotel on our own. But not until we had roll call. Twice.

I think Mr. Pettigrew was worried about losing somebody and I can't say I blamed him. If we'd lost someone in Tokyo it might have been a long time until they were found. And most of us hadn't slept very much on the flight, so we were pretty clueless after we got off the plane. So he made sure we were focused — on him — as we headed off in the direction where we'd get on the subway train that would take us to downtown Tokyo. I noticed the parent supervisors were especially watchful right then and, to be honest, I was okay with that.

Getting *to* the subway station was the easy part. Things got tougher after that. The maps in the subway stations looked like the blueprints for a space station. And I have to admit that, as we stood staring at the map, the one thought I had was Lorelei's comment when we'd first been thinking about Japan as our destination, that people here spoke Japanese. And we didn't. Except for Zaina and me, and I was pretty sure our minimal knowledge wasn't going to help much with the subway-travel issue.

Lorelei was busy reminding all of us that this was: "Exactly what I was worried about."

"This is an airport, Lorelei," I said to her. "It's not too late for you to go to England. They speak English there. You can catch a plane right here. We'll see you back at school in a couple of weeks."

Some kids laughed, but most didn't. I think they were still trying to adjust — I know I was — to a way of life that was about as different from what we knew back in Trimble as it was possible to be. A few of them were on cellphones calling their parents to let them knew we'd arrived safely in Tokyo.

Japan was going to take some getting used to. So many people, I know I already said that but there were SO MANY PEOPLE. And a transportation system that pretty much blew all of us away. But it wasn't long before we made our first discovery about Japan (other than how big and crowded it is). If you stare at the subway map long enough, eventually someone (sometimes more than one someone) will come along and help you figure out how to get where you want to go.

That's what happened right then. A man in a business suit and carrying a briefcase, and an older lady pulling a small suitcase on wheels approached us to offer help. The man bowed. I'd read about that Japanese courtesy but it was very cool when I saw it for the first time. He did not speak English, but Zaina and I, with our limited Japanese, managed to explain that we needed to get to the Shinjuku York Hotel and weren't sure just how to do that.

He was doing his best with a lot of pointing, gestures, and words that neither Zaina nor I understood, when the lady with the suitcase joined the conversation. She spoke English as well as any of us (better than Lorelei) and between the two of them, they were able to explain what we needed to know. We'd have to change trains a couple of times, but it turned out the businessman would be switching trains at the same station as our first transfer. He offered to make sure we got off at the right place and onto the right train for the second leg of our journey. Mr. Pettigrew nodded and thanked both people for the help.

There was another person, too. A girl, younger than us, was standing near the subway map, watching us. At first I thought she must be with the man or the lady who were assisting us. But as we all moved off in the direction of the trains, she stayed behind, alone.

I'm not even sure why I noticed her. Maybe it was because she was watching us so intently. Or was it just me she was watching? She didn't move or smile.

She was wearing what looked like a school uniform — not new and not a real nice one. It was neat and clean but looked sort of worn and the brown was faded.

She hadn't moved. And still she was looking in our direction.

I wondered if maybe she had never seen people from North America before. But that didn't make sense. This was Tokyo, not the African jungle. There'd be people from all over the world who lived in the city and thousands more who visited each year.

I'd fallen a bit behind so I turned and hurried to catch up with Zaina and the businessman, not really wanting to be the one who got lost in Tokyo. When I looked back again, the girl was gone. I figured her parents or a big brother or somebody had called her and she'd gone off to join them.

Something else we learned very quickly about life in Japan … something I thought was cool. People don't talk on their cellphones on the subway. Maybe not *never*, but very seldom. Lots of people will use their phones — there were people texting and reading stuff on their phones. And in an emergency, or for something critical, someone will make or take a call. But even then it's quick and the phone is off again. You won't hear the loud businessman closing some deal or the annoying junior-high kid planning the weekend's fun. Doesn't happen.

Mr. Wanaka, the Japanese gentleman who was helping us, was able to explain to Zaina and me that in Japan talking on your cell on the subway is considered rude. And as we were to learn during our time in Japan, being rude is like *the* biggest sin to the Japanese. Courtesy is a way of life.

Mr. Pettigrew told us that we were visitors to this country and would adhere to the local customs as much as possible. Lorelei was the only one to pull out her phone and Mr. Pettigrew made her put it away. Maybe she didn't know what *adhere* meant.

After about forty-five minutes, we arrived at our hotel and got checked into our rooms — I was assigned to share a room with Riley Repp. His twin brother, Jonathon, had not wanted to come on the trip, which I thought was odd. While we were unpacking our stuff I asked Riley about it.

"My parents are sort of weird, I guess. Ever since Jon and I were little, they always tried to make us think like two individual kids instead of like twins. They wouldn't let us dress the same, even if we wanted to, and they even made us have different haircuts."

I wasn't at all sure the Repps' parents were weird.

"So when he said he didn't want to be part of the Travel Club they were all cool with that."

"Well, it's a good thing he didn't come on the trip," I said. "That would have made an uneven number of boys."

"Yeah." Riley grinned. "You would have had to share a room with Lorelei Faber. Lucky you."

That triggered a pillow fight, the first of several Riley and I would have in Japan. We were in mid-battle when there was a knock at the door. It was Mr. Pettigrew telling us to be down in the lobby in fifteen minutes for dinner.

I washed my face and changed my T-shirt since the one I had on was sweaty after the pillow fight. We were on the fifteenth floor of the hotel. Riley wanted to take the stairs and I wanted to ride the elevator. A staircase in a strange building in a city I didn't know — I didn't think that was a great idea. Riley's argument was that we should be trying to stay in shape.

I told him that I was all about fitness, but that I'd heard that the Yakuza hung out in hotel stairwells waiting to kidnap unsuspecting victims.

"What's the Yakuza?"

"The Japanese mafia," I told him. "Except deadlier."

We took the elevator.

When we got off on the main floor, most of the kids and Mr. Pettigrew were already there. We had to wait for Lorelei and her roommate, Leah McAneely, a tenth-grade girl I didn't really know. Waiting for Lorelei and Leah would become a recurring theme throughout the trip.

When we stepped out of the hotel, it was nighttime. But the only way you would know that was by checking your watch. I thought I'd seen neon lights and cities that are pretty brightly lit at night. But I'd never seen anything like Shinjuku, which was the part of Tokyo where our hotel was located.

The Travel Club had showed the movie *Lost in Translation* once we'd decided on Japan as our destination. The first scene shows Bill Murray arriving in Tokyo at night. I don't know if the area he was looking at through the window of his taxi was Shinjuku or not but if it wasn't, it was very similar.

Two things happen when you walk down a major Shinjuku street at night. One, like I said, is that it's totally light. As bright as the sunniest day ever. The second is that you spend the whole time looking around, trying to take it all in. Which, by the way, is impossible.

Zaina and I were doing our best, our necks craned backwards and our eyes zipping first this way, then that. We were holding hands, but it wasn't a romantic thing so much as not wanting to get separated from each other. Or the group. I noticed Mr. Pettigrew wasn't looking at the lights and signs that were everywhere. He was watching us, making sure no one fell behind or wandered off. One thing I figured out really quickly — teachers on school trips don't spend much time being tourists.

Mr. Pettigrew hit a home run with his choice of the first restaurant of our trip. At least I thought so. It was called the Robot and we were greeted at the door by, you guessed it — a robot. But that was just the start of what would be one of the weirdest nights of my life.

The restaurant was sort of a midway funhouse. Times ten. The place looked like it was decorated by a genius artist while he was very drunk. Pulsing, flashing neon, huge mirrors, loud music, it was totally wild.

I leaned over to Zaina and yelled over the music, "I've never done LSD but I'm thinking this is it, right here."

She yelled back. "I have and this is crazier."

I looked at her and she giggled

She laughed. "Gotcha!"

I nodded and laughed, too.

While we were eating there was this endless show going on all around us … the performers playing huge drums, riding robot animals, firing lasers everywhere. The noise, the lights, the food smells — most people have five senses and trust me, the Robot didn't miss any of them.

Oh, and there was the food. Since none of us could read the menu, it was mostly a matter of pointing. Most of us ordered Bento boxes filled with rice, sushi, meat, and vegetables. I was guessing Lorelei passed on the Bento box but she was too far away for me to be able to tell for sure.

The show went on for about an hour and a half and it was amazing, but the nonstop energy — coupled with the major jetlag I was feeling — kind of wore me out as I watched it. I looked around and I think everybody was feeling the same way. When it was over, I'm pretty sure every one of us just wanted to get back to our hotel and get into bed.

Riley and I were too tired to even think about a pillow fight. But the weird thing is that once I was in bed I couldn't sleep, at least not right away. So, for twenty minutes or maybe half an hour, I lay there staring up into the darkness.

Between the travel and Shinjuku and the Robot, our first day in Japan was fairly unforgettable. That was my last thought before sleep finally took over and all that was left was a mind-picture of the young girl at the airport.

When we got down to the lobby the next morning, the two people I least expected to see were already there. Lorelei Faber and Leah McAneely were sitting on one of the big leather chesterfields. They were eating pizza.

First of all, it was 8:20 in the morning. Who eats pizza at 8:20 in the morning? And secondly, where do you buy pizza at 8:20 in the morning … in Tokyo?

To find out meant I would have had to actually have a conversation with Lorelei and that was something I didn't want to do at 8:20 in the morning. Or any other time of the day, come to think of it.

Mr. Pettigrew had a rule that none of us was allowed to leave the hotel on our own. And since I didn't see a pizza cart cruising the lobby, I figured Lorelei had broken one of the rules already.

Maybe she was worried that I might point that out to Mr. Pettigew because she offered both Riley and me a slice of pizza. I said no thanks and Riley did quite a good pantomime of someone barfing.

Lorelei was about to say something that I didn't expect to be all that pleasant when the elevator door opened and Mr. Pettigrew and a bunch of kids came into the lobby.

At least six people all said at about the same time, "Where'd you get the pizza?" So it was impossible for Mr. Pettigrew to ignore the issue.

He looked at Lorelei but before he could say anything, she pointed at this little old guy who was standing by the desk smiling at us. He bowed to Mr. Pettigrew, who returned the courtesy.

I knew exactly what had happened. Lorelei Faber, rich kid, had paid the man to go out and get her a pizza. That still didn't answer the question of where at that hour you'd find a pizza place but the guy over by the desk obviously knew.

Mr. Pettigrew gathered us all together and led us down a long hallway off the lobby to a room that was called the Heiwa Room. I only knew that because there was a sign that had both the Japanese and English names just to the right of the door (the English word was *harmony*).

We went inside and there was a long table all set up for breakfast and along the far wall was another table that had toast, juice, eggs, cereal — it was a breakfast you could get in a Motel 6 in North America and I think all of us were okay with that.

I wanted to try Japanese cuisine, but I also wanted to ease into it. Judging from the way everybody attacked the food table, it was obvious most of them felt the same way. As we ate, most of the kids were talking; some were on their phones texting. I wasn't doing either. In fact I wasn't even doing much eating.

I was feeling impatient. Not bored. In fact, even though we'd been in Japan less than twenty-four hours, I was already loving the place, especially the people.

But I was antsy. And I knew why. My reason for being in Japan was different from every other person in the group. I'd come here on a mission. The trouble was that I didn't really know what the mission was. Or how I was going to go about accomplishing it.

What I did know was that this school trip wasn't really going to begin, at least for me, until we reached Hiroshima. Where almost three-quarters of a century before, my great-grandfather had been part of a project that resulted in hundreds of thousands of people suffering and dying horribly.

What was it Carson had said? *There's nothing you can do that's going to change what happened seventy years ago. Or make things better.*

Maybe he was right. But wishing I could change history — that wasn't my reason for being here, I knew that much. Now if I could just figure out what *was* my reason for being here, life would be good. I'd have to work on that.

But not right now. Right now I was in a very cool part of a very cool city and I was going to learn all I could about this place and these people. And enjoy the moment. The "mission" would have to wait a few days.

I reached for a bowl of grapes.

As we were swallowing the last of our toast and fruit, a man came into the room and talked for a few minutes with Mr. Pettigrew. Then Mr. Pettigrew stood up and got our attention.

"Listen up, everyone." He clapped his hands together a couple of times. "Today's a big day. This is Mr. Tomai. He is a former teacher and will be our guide for the next few days. You will call him Tomai-*sensei*, which is a way of showing respect for an elder who is also a teacher. And I know how much all of you like to show respect for your teachers."

We all laughed at that and Mr. Pettigrew smiled. I noticed Tomai-*sensei's* expression didn't change, but he bowed to Mr. Pettigrew then to us.

"There will be a bus outside the hotel in —" Mr. Pettigrew looked at his watch "— twenty minutes. You just have time to go back to your rooms, do what you have to do to get ready, and be downstairs in exactly twenty minutes." He drew out the word *exactly*.

"We'll be gone all day so bring everything you think you'll need for the day. And you might want to bring jackets. It's supposed to rain today and we will be outside at least some of the time."

Eighteen minutes later, Riley and I walked off the elevator, through the lobby of the hotel and out to the waiting bus where Mr. Pettigrew and Tomai-*sensei* were standing. Both of them nodded to us as we stepped on the bus. A lot of people were already on the bus and a bunch more were right behind us as we boarded.

I sat down next to Zaina, and Riley sat with Devonne Chelf. We'd worked that out the day before and everybody was good with the arrangement. That, of course, didn't stop kids from giving Zaina and me a fair amount of *Hey, it's the lovebirds* kind of razzing but we didn't mind.

Actually the razzing was less than usual because Lorelei and Leah weren't on the bus yet. Five minutes after our twenty-minute deadline had passed they still weren't on the bus. And when they did finally arrive — five minutes after that — they were the only two people who weren't carrying jackets.

But finally we were off. Our first stop was Asakusa, an area I thought was amazing.

It's famous for Senso-ji, a Buddhist temple that dates back to the seventh century and for a shopping area with a large street leading to the temple. Running off from the main street were a bunch of tiny little streets — walkways, really — with tons of cool shops that were more like little kiosks. We cruised them for a while and I bought a scarf for my mom and another one for my sister. They were pretty nice scarves and I thought about getting something different — and cheaper — for my sister, but decided to stick with the scarf.

I looked for something for my dad and Carson, but didn't see anything I thought they'd really like. As we were coming out of one of the tiny streets back into the larger street, a group of actors began performing something that Tomai-*sensei* told us was called kabuki. It's a form of theatre with a lot of dance mixed in. The performers dress in pretty bizarre costumes and have what I would call *extreme* makeup. It was all telling a story, but I can't say I understood too much of it even with Tomai-*sensei* explaining and doing some interpreting.

Still I thought it was pretty amazing and I could have watched longer, but after maybe fifteen minutes, some of the kids (can you say Lorelei Faber?) wanted to do something else. But just as we were getting ready to leave, there was some commotion over by the temple. We looked over and noticed that a wedding party had arrived.

Zaina pulled me in that direction. "I want to see this," she told me.

She wasn't alone. Most of the kids started working their way toward the wedding party. We wanted to get as close as we could to see what a Japanese wedding was like.

The bride was beautiful. She was wearing what I would say was part dress, part fur coat, both white, and on her head was a tall triangular head piece that was huge and spectacular. Everything moved very slowly and there was a lot of ritual. It all seemed quite solemn but as we got closer I could see that both the bride and groom were smiling and looked very happy. Once the couple moved up into the temple, Mr. Pettigrew gathered us up and we headed again for the little bus that was our mode of travel.

I turned — and there she was. The girl from the airport.

I was sure it was her. But then I was just as sure that it *couldn't* be the same girl; I had to be wrong. It didn't make any sense that she just happened to show up at two different places we were at.

But if it wasn't the same girl then it was two different girls who looked very much alike and this girl, like the first one, was staring intently at us. And that made even less sense.

I tried to get a look at what she was wearing to see if it was the same faded brown uniform. But she was behind a planter and I could only see her head and shoulders. It was almost like she was hiding.

The spooky part was that what she was doing was more than just watching. There's watching someone, and there's, I don't know, stalking someone. Which, I told myself, was crazy.

It was like she wanted to come over and talk to us but was too shy. And since I was the only kid not yet on the bus, it seemed like maybe it was me she wanted to speak to. I watched her for a couple of minutes and finally decided to go over and say something to her. "Let's go, Christian," Mr. Pettigrew said. "We still have a lot of ground to cover today."

I nodded and started after him but I stopped and look back one more time at the young girl. She was still looking at me but there was no more time and I climbed on the bus. I slid in next to Zaina, who was texting.

"Did you see that girl out there?"

"What girl?"

I pointed with my chin. "Over there."

We both looked.

"I don't see anyone."

The girl had disappeared.

"She was there a minute ago," I said.

Zaina shrugged. "Maybe, but she's not there now."

I sat back on my seat. "She was maybe ten or eleven," I said. "And it looked like she wanted to come over and talk to me. But she didn't."

"I wonder why she isn't in school."

"Good point." I hadn't thought of that. "She had a school uniform on — at least I think that's what it was."

"Maybe she just fell for your rugged good looks," Zaina laughed.

I grinned at her. "That happens a lot so that's probably it."

"I wonder why it didn't happen to me."

"Ha, ha." But then I turned serious. "It was weird. I was so sure she wanted to say something to me but we never got the chance to talk to each other."

"How's your Japanese?"

Another good point. Maybe she didn't speak English and that's why she hadn't spoken to me.

"In some countries tourists get approached a lot by young kids and usually they're begging."

"I know but I don't think that happens in Japan. And she didn't look like a beggar."

Zaina went back to her texting while I craned my neck to look out the window as the bus worked its way through the narrow streets around Asakusa but I didn't see the mystery girl again.

CHAPTER
FIFTEEN

Some people had thought Asakusa was boring and were making comments while we headed for our next stop.

If it was action they craved, they were about to get it.

We were on our way to Shibuya Crossing. I remembered it from *Lost in Translation*. It's like Times Square on steroids. I'd done some Googling as well and knew that Shibuya Crossing is a scramble intersection where all of the traffic is stopped in every direction at the same time. That's when all the pedestrians cross at once, coming from every direction, and *going* in every direction. During the busiest times more than 2,500 people are all crossing at the same time while all around them are amazing buildings, huge television screens, and a bazillion or so high-tech electronic signs.

Mr. Pettigrew took us to a Starbucks that was on the second floor of one of the buildings that overlooked Shibuya Crossing. We all drank our coffees and caramel macchiatos and watched the mayhem unfold below us every couple of minutes.

We finished our drinks and it was time for us to try it. A lot of teachers wouldn't have taken a bunch of kids down into a place that was as crowded and crazy as Shibuya, but Mr. Pettigrew was all about us trying new stuff. He and the parent supervisors made their way to different corners of the crossing. Then it was our turn. Some of us, including Zaina and me, crossed a few times — going first one way and then back the other way.

I know it sounds dumb but every time I crossed that street I looked around for the girl I'd seen in Asakusa and at the airport. But I didn't see her.

Eventually we all ended up at this huge statue of a dog named Hachiko, which is at one corner of Shibuya Crossing. The dog's owner was a professor and every day Hachiko would meet him when he got off the train at Shibuya Station. But one day in 1925 the professor died and did not return to the station. For nine years, nine months, and fifteen days until his own death, Hachiko came to the station at the time the professor had always returned from work and waited for his master's appearance. It was kind of sad and as we stood there looking at the statue, I could see tears in Zaina's eyes.

Lorelei said, "That must have been one dumb dog." If I'd never met Lorelei before, that would have told me all I needed to know about her.

The third part of our day was also excellent. For two reasons. First of all, it rained. Not a cold rain or even an uncomfortable rain ... unless you weren't wearing a jacket. Which two girls on our tour were not.

Lorelei and Leah kept ducking into doorways trying to get out of the rain. But Mr. Pettigrew — with maybe just a hint of an evil smile on his face — kept moving us along.

"Come on people, we've got places to get to — can't be standing around."

Since there were only two people standing around, we all knew who he was talking to. The rain lasted about an hour and in that time I think the two jacketless girls may have set a new world record for whining and complaining.

This is stupid, we could die out here, you know.

and

If I get pneumonia, my mother is so going to sue you.

But the best was when Lorelei pointed to a restaurant. "I'm hungry. I'm going in there and you better be out here when I come out."

"Go ahead, Lorelei." Mr. Pettigrew nodded. "You go right into that sushi restaurant and have some nice lunch. You can catch up with us when you're finished eating your Japanese food. We'll all be at the big pizza place up in the next block."

That shut the two whiners up for a while — until they realized there was no pizza place in the next block or the block after that.

Several people had brought along umbrellas. Needless to say, Lorelei and Leah weren't among them. Zaina was. After we'd been walking for quite a while, Lorelei sped up and got close up behind Zaina and me.

"It's not really right, you know."

"What isn't right, Lorelei?" I thought about doing my nasal impersonation of her annoying voice but thought that might be a little nasty.

"You guys have, like, jackets *and* an umbrella. You don't need both."

"So what are you suggesting, Lorelei?" I think Zaina was enjoying Lorelei's discomfort as much as I was.

"I'll give you five bucks for your jacket."

"What?"

"Not to buy it. Just to use it. Just for, like, today."

"I don't think my jacket would fit you, Lorelei," Zaina said.

"I'll rent you mine," I said.

"Okay," Lorelei's face lit up like a department store Christmas tree. "Here." She held out her money.

I shook my head. "But not for five bucks."

"How much?" She put her chubby hands on her chubby hips and glared at me.

"Four hundred dollars," I said and turned away.

"You stupid … stupid …"

I could tell she wanted to call me something … uh … unladylike … but Mr. Pettigrew wasn't far away and she decided not to go there.

"Okay … ten bucks," I said.

"Deal." Lorelei couldn't get the other five out fast enough.

And the best part? The rain stopped a few minutes after that. Lorelei demanded her money back.

"Sorry, a deal's a deal," I said. "But I'll tell you what: you can wear the jacket for the rest of the day."

"I don't want your crappy jacket, you ... dork." And she threw the jacket at me. I was pretty sure *crappy* and *dork* weren't the words she wanted to use but again Mr. Pettigrew was too close for Lorelei to use some of her more colourful phrases.

The third stop of the day was also cool. The Tokyo Skytree is the tallest tower in the world. It's a radio and television broadcasting tower but it also has a restaurant and three observation decks, including the one at the top that is 634 metres or 2,080 feet off the ground. Of course, all of us wanted to go to the very top where the observation deck has a glass floor that people can stand on and look straight down at the street below.

Now I know that sounds totally amazing to most people and I thought it would be pretty cool to go up there but once we were there — whoa. A lot of the kids couldn't wait to get out on the glass floor but there were two of us who had a little trouble with the idea. Me and ... Lorelei Faber.

I could tell Lorelei was afraid of heights because her face was the colour of two percent milk. Mine probably wasn't much better. But I didn't want anyone to know so I kind of edged my way out onto the nearest edge of the platform. What I didn't do was look down. Instead I looked at Zaina as I squeezed her hand so hard I'm sure I crushed a few bones.

She didn't yelp or even say anything. But she knew.

"Well, this is great," she said after a minute or so, "but I think I've had enough." And she pulled me inside off the platform. That's when I saw Lorelei. And for the first time ever I didn't feel like saying anything smartass to her. I've seen scared before but the absolute terror in Lorelei's eyes was something I had never seen.

Her roommate, Leah, and a couple of other kids were yelling for her to come out on the platform. Lorelei was too numb to even answer them and right away a couple of kids started rolling their eyes and snickering. They were smart enough not to actually say anything, but I could see what they were thinking.

That's when Zaina did something I wish I'd thought of. She turned to Lorelei and said real loud. "Thanks for going out there with me. I don't think I'd have done it if you weren't right there beside me."

And I guess because everybody had been looking down all the time they were out there, they didn't realize that Lorelei hadn't actually set foot on the glass platform. Anyway, the eye-rolling and the snickering turned to shrugs and kids refocused on the ground below them. *Way* below them.

It wasn't until we were back on the ground, two-fifths of a mile below that glass platform that anybody said anything much.

Lorelei walked off a little ways from the group and gestured at Zaina to follow her over there. I ambled along. I wanted to hear Lorelei Faber say thank you with my own ears. I was pretty sure it had never happened before.

"What did you do that for?" Lorelei glared at Zaina.

Zaina smiled. "I didn't think you wanted people to know you were scared to go out on that platform."

"Yeah, well, just so you know, I wasn't afraid to go out there. I just thought it was stupid. Totally juvenile. Who wants to stand on a hunk of glass and look at their feet? Duh."

Zaina looked stunned by the words. She didn't know Lorelei as well as I did. Nothing that came from those jiggly jowls could surprise me.

"Yeah," I said. "Anybody could tell you weren't scared, Lorelei. In fact, I bet if we went back up there right now you'd be just as not scared as before — probably want to race right out there. Except that it's so darn juvenile."

Zaina took my hand and squeezed it. I think she was telling me to shut up.

"Sorry, Lorelei," she said. "I just thought —"

"Nobody asked you to think." Lorelei's eyes were little hate-slits as she snarled the words. "So next time just mind your own business and keep your mouth shut."

She stomped off. I watched her go and when she got back to Leah and the others I could hear her nasally twang. "Wasn't that a blast? I could have stayed up there all day. Such a gorgeous view. When are we going to get something to eat? I'm starving over here."

Mr. Pettigrew looked over at Zaina and me and I'm pretty sure he knew because he shrugged. Just a little shrug, but a shrug just the same.

I loved our time in Tokyo. It was an amazing city with so much energy and excitement that none of us wanted to leave.

The next day we'd be heading off to Hiroshima and with every passing minute I found myself getting more excited. And anxious. What if Zaina and Carson were right? What if there was nothing I could do that would matter at all?

Part of me couldn't wait to get that part of the trip started, but another part of me was worried that it might be a total disappointment. A complete waste of time. That I'd get there and — as much as I wanted to see where they had actually dropped the bomb my great-grandfather had helped create — the whole thing might be a big letdown. What if when we left in a week I didn't know any more than I knew now?

That night when we were back at the hotel, I asked Mr. Pettigrew if Zaina and I could go for a short walk. I promised that we wouldn't go far or leave the main streets around the hotel and that we wouldn't be gone long.

"Sorry," he replied, shaking his head. "I can't let you do that, Christian, but here's what I'll do. Once I'm sure everyone is in their rooms the three of us will go for a walk. You two go ahead and I'll stay back. I promise I won't be watching you the whole time and you don't need to hurry or think you have to get right back because I'm there. You can have your walk, but not without me back there somewhere."

I wanted to argue, but I could see why he couldn't just let us go off by ourselves. So I nodded. "Okay, thanks."

I told Zaina about my chat with Mr. Pettigrew and we agreed to meet in the lobby in a half hour. I went to my room and while Riley Repp watched Japanese baseball on TV, I sent off a couple of texts, one to Carson — I figured he'd love the Lorelei/Skytree story — and one to my parents.

Sometimes, or maybe most of the time, things don't turn out quite the way you planned them. That was one of those nights. A few other kids felt the same way Zaina and I did and also wanted to go for a walk on their last night in Tokyo. I couldn't really blame them. It meant Zaina and I wouldn't be alone, but it was fine. The more energetic kids kind of moved ahead of us anyway, pointing at stuff and taking selfies and talking loud.

Zaina and I hung back and although we were looking at stuff, too — it was hard not to in Shinjuku — neither of us said anything at first. Zaina asked me a couple of times if I was okay, mostly, I guess, because I wasn't talking.

"I'm fine, really," I told her. "I'm just thinking about some things."

One of the cool things about Zaina was that she was okay with us not talking to each other all the time. So that night we walked a lot and held hands and looked at things and didn't say a lot.

But there was one thing I wanted to ask her. We'd just started back toward the hotel and I turned to her.

"Do you believe in ghosts?"

She looked at me and her shoulders went up a little bit. "I don't know … I guess so. Sort of."

I laughed. "Not a very definite answer."

"I know." She smiled. "What about you?"

I didn't reply right away.

"I was thinking about that girl I saw at Asakusa. What if — what if she was a ghost?"

"The girl at Asakusa? You think she might have been a ghost?"

"I don't know," I said. "I mean I know it sounds crazy but it was kind of spooky, you know, she showed up and then she was gone and then there she was again."

"You didn't tell me you saw her twice."

I nodded. "I saw her at the airport, too. I mean I'm pretty sure it was the same person."

"*Pretty* sure," Zaina repeated.

"Yeah." We started walking again. "Listen, I know it sounds weird and I don't blame you if you think I've lost it. But think about this … this is Japan. So many people died here in the war. And lots of them were kids. Like her. Like us. I just think …" I stopped mostly because I wasn't sure *what* I thought. Or what I wanted to say. All I knew was that whatever I said would probably sound lame — even to me.

"But why would a ghost want to appear to us?"

"She didn't appear to *us* … or them." I waved my arm in the direction of the other kids walking ahead of us. "She appeared to me."

"Okay, now you're creeping me out."

"Sorry," I said. "I mean, if she is a ghost, I don't think she wants to do anything bad or evil, nothing like that. I think she just wants to communicate with … I guess with me."

"Then why didn't she?"

I thought about that. "I'm not sure. Maybe because there were too many people around."

For a few minutes we walked without saying anything. I tried to sort it out in my mind. What was weirder — some kind of spirit presence or a girl who had showed up twice at two different places that she couldn't possibly have known we'd be at. Of course, there was one more possibility — that I was so excited (what my parents call "overstimulated") that I'd hallucinated — dreamed the whole thing, that there *was* no girl except in my mind.

We'd caught up to the rest of the group so I lowered my voice and leaned in toward Zaina.

"Anyway," I said, "thanks for letting me talk about this. I was afraid you'd think I was a total loser and —"

Zaina looked around, then pulled me into a doorway. "I think you should kiss me," she said.

Which, all things considered, seemed like a really good idea. And for the next minute I didn't think about mystery girls or anything other than the girl I was kissing.

We stepped back out of the doorway and I looked back. Mr. Pettigrew had stopped and looked like he was totally interested in the sidewalk. Cool guy, Pettigrew.

On the way back to the hotel, I looked at Zaina and said again, "Thanks."

She laughed. "For kissing you?"

"No. For not thinking I've lost my mind."

"Actually," she said. "I'm pretty sure you *have* lost your mind. I just always wanted to kiss a nut case." She punched me softly in the arm.

And we both laughed.

Later when I was lying in bed staring up into the darkness and listening to Riley Repp's rhythmic breathing in the next bed, I tried to go over in my mind the thoughts I'd been having since I found out about Great-Grandpa Will.

It had been easy back in Trimble to think that once I got to Japan everything would fall into place and I'd just magically stumble into something I could do that would show the world that the Deavers and Larkins are okay. And everything would be fine in the universe again.

But from the minute we got off the plane at Narita Airport, I'd been having different thoughts. Doubts. Maybe it *was* crazy to think that a kid would go to Hiroshima seventy years after the bomb happened and do something that actually mattered.

I probably would have lain there wide awake for a long time, but my phone let me know I'd received a text. I got up and read it. It was from Carson.

> I've decided to marry Lorelei. I've really been worrying a lot lately about marrying someone I'd get bored with. I don't think life would ever be dull with "L." I'll ask her as soon as you guys get back.

It was the perfect text at exactly the right time. I'm pretty sure I was still laughing when I fell asleep a few minutes later.

CHAPTER SIXTEEN

Even with all the doubts I had, I was the first one in the lobby the next morning. In fact, for the first while I was by myself except for Tomai-*sensei*, who was sitting very upright in one of the big chairs. He nodded and said good morning.

I sat in another chair opposite him. He didn't seem to want to chat — Tomai-*sensei* wasn't a chatty guy — so I pulled the book I'd been reading — *Butter* by Erin Lange — out of my backpack. I opened it, stared at the page for a few minutes and put it back in the backpack.

I was too restless to sit and read. I stood up and looked out the window at the street that was already filling with people going in every direction. I turned, leaned against a pillar, and watched as kids dragged their suitcases and stuff off the elevator and into the lobby. Most of them looked hungry and sleepy.

A few also looked grumpy, which often goes along with hungry and sleepy. Lorelei was the last one, lagging maybe ten or fifteen steps behind everybody else. But not lagging at all in the grumpy department.

Her lips were moving. There was no one near her so I guessed she was talking to herself. I was pretty sure what she was saying didn't sound anything like, "Oh, what a beautiful morning." Which, come to think of it, is a song. Yeah, Lorelei wasn't singing.

Mr. Pettigrew was the opposite of grumpy in the morning. Every morning. At school and here in Japan. He was one of those people who looked at every day like a new adventure. Not all teachers seemed to look at the world that way. Probably from having to teach the Loreleis of the world.

Mr. Pettigrew gathered everybody around him. Some sat on the floor; some perched on the arms of sofas and giant armchairs. Lorelei sprawled on a couch and yawned loudly. Mr. Pettigrew and the rest of us ignored her.

"Another new experience for us today. As you know, we are off to Hiroshima. What you may not know is how we're going to get there." He paused. I think he was wanting a little dramatic effect there.

"We'll be travelling by train," he continued. "But not just any train. This one is called the Shinkansen. English people call it the 'Bullet Train,' which is not, I'm told, an exact translation, but is a pretty good description. First of all, it looks like a bullet. And secondly it is fast, very fast. At times we will be traveling at speeds up to three hundred and twenty kilometres per hour or two hundred miles per hour."

Riley Repp and Devonne Chelf high-fived and a couple of people fist-pumped. I smiled at Zaina who was across the room and she raised her eyebrows.

"We'll be on the Shinkansen for four hours," Mr. Pettigrew said. "So I need you to stick together. You can move around some, but you won't be able to roam all over the train. We're taking the subway to get to the train station, so no loitering, Ms. Faber, and I hope all of you remembered everything in your rooms."

There was a lot of patting pockets and opening backpacks, but nobody went screaming back to the elevators in a panic.

"We will follow Tomai-*sensei*. Let's go."

Zaina sidled up and gave me the smile I was getting to like more every day.

"Do you think they have seat belts on this train?" she wondered.

"At two hundred miles an hour, I'm not sure it would matter."

"Oh well, that makes me feel a lot better."

Okay, two words. Mount Fuji.

I'd checked it online just like I had the Shibuya Crossing. There is no way an online photograph comes close to the real thing. It was amazing to watch it out the window of the Shinkansen. (Which from now on I'm going to refer to as the "Bullet Train" because it's easier to write.)

I'd hoped we'd be able to see Mount Fuji when we were at the top of the Skytree but it was cloudy that day and the famous mountain was invisible to us. So it was pretty special to see it now. Everybody had their phones out (a couple of people had actual cameras) and were snapping pictures like crazy as we zipped along in the train.

Zaina was relieved to learn that the Bullet Train actually does have seatbelts. In fact, it's more like being on a plane than anything else with rows of seats on both sides of an aisle that runs down the middle. Except for in the dining car. Which was very cool. Glass tables with four seats, two on each side on one side of the aisle, and a table for two on the other side.

There was only one problem with the dining car. No dining. It didn't actually have food. They'd phased out the dining cars a couple of years ago. In fact, we learned that most of the trains didn't have dining cars anymore but the one we were on hadn't refitted the dining car for regular seating yet.

But Mr. Pettigrew had all that handled for us. He'd purchased snacks and bento boxes and sandwiches at the station before we'd left and he and the parents passed them out to us as we sat in the non-dining car.

I thought about asking Lorelei if she wanted to stand on one of the glass tables to practise for our next trip to the Skytree but I knew it would bother Zaina if I did so I kept my mouth shut.

Lorelei did not keep her mouth shut. Especially when she saw the food choices. She settled on a sandwich of some kind and some chips. No sense going all crazy on getting into the Japanese culture.

When we'd eaten and made our way back to our seats in the regular car, Zaina asked one of the attendants for a pillow. She curled up and went to sleep, her head against my shoulder.

I couldn't sleep and didn't want to. This was the part of the trip I'd been thinking about since I'd first suggested Japan to the Travel Club. We were only hours away from the place where one of the worst man-made catastrophes in the history of the world had happened.

Something my great-grandfather was a part of. And I had still this crazy idea that I could do something to right at least a little bit of the wrong.

I thought about that. I thought about GG Will, the smartest guy and the coolest guy ever. I thought about what it must have been like — all these scientists working day after day, month after month, to create a weapon unlike anything ever seen before.

And I thought about Hiroshima.

CHAPTER SEVENTEEN

I hadn't slept a lot the night before — mostly thinking about what the next few days would bring. I guess that's why I fell asleep on the train. When I woke up and looked around we were pulling into the station in Hiroshima. The sky was an amazing blue and it looked warm.

Mr. Pettigrew stood and turned to face us. "And what's the single phrase I've repeated most during this trip?"

Several of us answered, "Make sure you have all your stuff."

"Excellent. Gather your gear and be ready. Tomai-*sensei* will lead us. I understand we can walk to our hotel from here. He will lead; we will follow."

A couple of minutes later we were standing on the platform. I looked around. I know it sounds crazy but I guess I expected to see evidence of the bomb right away. I knew that the Shinkansen station we were at had been destroyed that day.

And I guess this sounds even crazier, but I actually felt a little disappointed when I didn't see any damage. In fact, what I did see — and would see a lot in the next few days — was a city that was really quite beautiful. There is a lot of water and several bridges in Hiroshima, rivers and an inland sea being part of the city.

"Doesn't look that bad to me."

The words came from Lorelei Faber and for a second I wanted to turn on her and say something like *what do you want — bodies on the sidewalks*? But, of course I didn't, mostly because I'd actually been thinking pretty much the same thing.

"I think we will have to imagine what it must have been like," said Zaina.

I nodded. "They've had seventy years to rebuild. It's not going to be anything like what it was right after the bomb."

But even as I was saying it I was sneaking a peak here and there hoping to spot a chunk of broken concrete here, a hole in a wall there.

"Let's go," Mr. Pettigrew called out and he and Tomai-*sensei* headed off toward the street. And we already knew that Tomai-*sensei* was a fast walker.

All of us shouldered backpacks, pulled handles out of suitcases, and hurried after the two adults.

Behind me I heard Lorelei's editorial comment.

"Oh, crap."

Carson was right. Being married to *L*, as he called her, would never be dull.

We had walked about four or five blocks and I kept swivelling my head around hoping to see the Hiroshima

Peace Memorial, also known as the Atomic Bomb Dome. It was a building that had been all but destroyed by the bomb. It has been a symbol of that day and one of the things I most wanted to see when we got to Hiroshima.

The bomb had exploded almost directly over it and everyone inside had been killed. But somehow the shell of the building stayed standing — like a metal-concrete skeleton rising above the rubble that was everywhere around it for two kilometres.

Of course Hiroshima is a huge city so the chances that we would see the Dome right after stepping off the train were remote. And we didn't.

I hoped it wasn't a sign that my wanting to do something important — something significant — wouldn't move ahead any farther than it had in Tokyo.

Zaina must have figured out what I was thinking. She leaned in to me and said, "Don't forget to enjoy the city. If what you want to happen happens, that's great, but in the meantime don't miss the rest of the reason why we're here."

It was good advice. I knew I was becoming kind of obsessed with the idea that I could actually do something that mattered. And that probably made me a pain in the butt to be around.

But I wasn't ready to let go of what I'd come here to do. Not yet. Zaina was right, though. I nodded.

"Okay, I get it," I said. "I promise to be the big bundle of fun you're crazy about."

She laughed. "Don't flatter yourself."

We both laughed then.

I was honestly trying to lighten up, but the truth was I had other things on my mind. Like how soon we were going to the Peace Park, which is where the Atomic Bomb Dome stands. I thought that maybe that's where my plan to do something to make up for GG Will's part in the bombing would start to take shape.

I'd have time to think about it, though, because Mr. Pettigrew announced that we would be going to the Peace Park in the morning. Which made sense — why go there with most of the day already gone? It didn't help my impatience any, though.

I would have been outvoted, anyway, because every kid in the group wanted food to be the number-one priority. And Mr. Pettigrew and Tomai-*sensei* collected huge brownie points that night as they took us to a place called the J-Café and Grill.

Where they served pasta.

I thought Lorelei was going to kiss Mr. Pettigrew, but she settled for saying, "Good call, Pettigrew-*sensei*." Every once in a while Lorelei came out with something really good. That, I had to admit, was *really* good.

And she was right. My ravioli went down pretty well.

We did some tourist stuff for the rest of that night: a garden and a temple and I'm sure they were both amazing but I just couldn't get into it. I didn't want to bring the others down so I pretended I was knocked out by all of it, but the truth was I just couldn't focus.

Until we were walking back to the hotel. That's when a passing passenger bus got my full attention. Actually it was someone *on* the bus that had me watching it as it rolled past us, turned a corner, and was gone.

I was sure — no, that's not true — I was *pretty* sure, that the only passenger on the bus was the girl I'd seen twice in Tokyo. She was sitting on the side closest to us and looking out the window. At us.

At me.

Zaina was also looking at me and I could tell she was wondering what I thought was so fascinating about a bus. But she didn't ask and I didn't tell her. I knew she hadn't seen the girl. Or maybe she *couldn't* see the girl. Anyway I didn't see the point of giving her another reason to think the guy she was going out with was a nutbar.

Later that night we got back to the hotel and all of us were moving toward the elevator when Mr. Pettigrew called me off to one side. When a teacher wants to talk to you, away from everyone else, it's kind of like when a cop looks at you or wants to talk to you. Even if it's just to wish you a Merry Christmas or something, there's this *Oh my God, what did I do?* feeling inside.

So when I got over to Mr. Pettigrew my mind was working overtime. Was this about the girl on the bus? Or had I done something wrong? I didn't think I'd insulted Lorelei … I hadn't left anything behind … I thought I'd paid for my ravioli … what could he possibly want?

Mr. Pettigrew looked at me for a moment and then said, "Christian, tomorrow we'll be going to the Peace Park and we'll see the Atomic Bomb Dome and the Children's Peace Monument. I hope the day is what you want it to be. Carson told me a little about your … quest.

I hope it works out. But if it doesn't, I hope you won't think this has all been for nothing."

It was almost a repeat of what Zaina had said. I didn't know how to answer him. I had no idea Mr. Pettigrew knew that I wasn't just here to be a tourist.

Finally I nodded. "Thanks, Mr. Pettigrew. No matter what happens tomorrow, this has been an amazing trip. I mean that."

He smiled. "Okay, better get up to your room. Early start tomorrow. They're feeding us down here at 7:30."

I nodded, turned and started for the elevator. But I turned back to him just as the elevator doors opened.

"Mr. Pettigrew, do you think I'm crazy?"

Mr. Pettigrew shook his head. "It's not crazy to want to do something positive. And it's never crazy to chase your dream."

I smiled. "Good night, sir."

"Good night, Chris."

Day 6 in Japan. Day 2 in Hiroshima.

The day I'd been waiting for … the day we'd go to the place that stands as a monument to what happened on August 6, 1945. It was quieter than usual on the bus on the way to the Peace Park. Usually there was a fair amount of loud talking and joshing around, but not today.

Before we left for Japan, Mr. Pettigrew had taken one of our travel meetings to talk about the war and the bombing of Hiroshima and Nagasaki. He talked about the thousands of people who died as a result of those bombs.

It seemed that the kids on the bus were thinking about some of the stuff Mr. Pettigrew had talked about in that meeting. Even Lorelei was quiet and looked like she was thinking about things.

We arrived at the Peace Park and our driver let us off at the end of the park farthest from the Atomic Bomb Dome which I could now see for the first time. We piled off the bus and Mr. Pettigrew gathered us around him.

"Okay, here's what we're going to do." He looked at his watch. "It's ten minutes to ten. I'm letting all of you go on your own to see the Peace Park. We will meet under the Children's Peace Monument — that's the place with all the paper cranes — at noon. I don't want anyone to be late for that and if you are, it will be the last time you will be allowed to wander on your own. Does everyone understand?"

There were nods and low murmurs from kids. We understood.

"One more thing," Mr. Pettigrew added. "The bomb exploded almost directly over where we are standing. This is a very important place, almost a sacred place to the Japanese people. We will conduct ourselves in a mature, respectful manner while we are here. Is that clear?"

More nods. For the first time I wasn't sure Mr. Pettigrew's warning was necessary. As I looked around at the faces of everyone in our group, they didn't look like people who were planning to get crazy or disrespectful.

"Tomai-*sensei* and the parents and I will circulate around the park. All of you have my cell number. Call me or text me if you need me for anything. And if there is anyone who is nervous about being by themselves, you are welcome to stay with me. I'll be going to all of the areas in the park that are important."

There were no takers on that idea and I'm pretty sure Mr. Pettigrew didn't expect any. He pointed to the Children's Peace Monument, which wasn't far from where we were standing. "That's where we meet. Twelve o'clock sharp. I'll see you then."

At first we kind of milled around for a while but then people started moving off in twos and threes. Zaina and I were the last ones to actually move. Part of it was I didn't know where I wanted to start.

I looked at Zaina and I guess she could see I was struggling. We were finally here and I couldn't seem to make my legs move.

She smiled at me. "I think we should start at the Dome even though it's at the far end of the park," she said, pointing. "Sound okay to you?"

"Sounds perfect to me." I nodded and we started working our way through and around the crowd of people that was everywhere. It wasn't long before we were standing directly below the Atomic Bomb Dome, the shell of the building that had been closest to where the bomb exploded.

I found myself looking up into the sky where a few hundred metres above this place, the bomb had exploded.

"It was government offices during the war," Zaina said. "There were about thirty people in the building that morning. None survived."

A fence encircled the building so we couldn't go inside or get right up to it. But I could still feel the power of being there — standing right there. And I could understand why this framework of a building meant so much to the Japanese people.

Zaina and I didn't talk much for the next hour. We walked, then stood, then walked some more — three or four times back and forth along the sidewalk that ran on one side of the Dome; finally we moved off toward another building that partly remained after the blast and had been restored afterwards.

It was called the Rest House and the main floor was an information area and gift shop. The basement was still the same as it was the morning of the bomb.

"Hard to believe that someone in there actually survived." Zaina shook her head.

"Seriously?"

Obviously Zaina had done a lot of reading before we got to Japan. I had, too, but I'd concentrated on the bomb itself because of GG Will. So it was cool having Zaina kind of like a guide during our walk through the Peace Park.

"He'd gone down to the basement to get some documents and the bomb exploded while he was down there. Everyone else died instantly but even though the building was pretty well destroyed and he was buried under wreckage, he survived, lived until he was in his eighties."

"You're right," I said, "that's hard to imagine."

Zaina nodded.

After we'd gone through the gift shop and bought a couple of souvenirs and taken some brochures from the information centre, we walked to an area that looked over the basement area. It had been kept exactly the way it had been after the bomb hit. We stood for a long time, just looking. There wasn't really anything to say. I'm not sure how long we stayed there before going back outside.

"Where to next?" Zaina asked me.

I looked around. "What about the Children's Peace Monument?"

"Good idea," she agreed.

This time Zaina gave me some of the story of the monument before we got to it. I knew some of it already but not all of it.

"There was a little girl who was two years old in 1945," Zaina told me. "She lived with her family a couple of kilometres from here. She was blown out of the house through a window. But she survived … wasn't really even injured very badly. But a few years later — I think she was about eleven — she got sick with leukemia that was caused by the radiation from the bomb. When she was in the hospital she started making these paper cranes because there was a belief that if you made a thousand cranes you could have a wish granted."

By now we were getting close to the monument and I could see a huge sort of tripod structure with the statue of a girl and crane on top.

"What happened to her?"

"Unfortunately, she died before she could finish making all the cranes," Zaina said softly, "but she wasn't forgotten and the cranes became symbols of peace. Ever since this monument was built a couple of years after she died, people bring or send millions of paper cranes to this place every year."

We stopped right below the three-legged pedestal and I read the words on the plaque that stood there.

> *This is our cry, This is our prayer, Peace in the World.*

Again we stayed there a long time, looking at the cranes that were everywhere and up at the statue, the girl's name was Sadako Sasaki. And I thought of the girl I'd seen ... *thought* I'd seen in Tokyo. Was she ...

I looked at Zaina. "I wish I had a crane to leave here."

"You do," Zaina smiled at me and opened her backpack. She took out two cranes and gave one to me.

I tried to say "Wow," but it came out kind of like I had something in my throat. Which I guess I did.

We laid our cranes at the bottom of one of the legs of the pedestal.

"You made these?" I looked at Zaina.

She nodded. "Uh-huh. One night in our hotel in Tokyo."

"Cool, you did a good job, these are really —"

But she wasn't looking at me. She was looking across the way to the other side of the monument.

I followed her eyes. To where Lorelei Faber was placing cranes very carefully on the pavement. She was looking down so she didn't see us.

Zaina took my hand and led me away.

"I don't think she'd want us to see her or know that she was doing that."

I waited until we got far enough away that I knew Lorelei couldn't see us. I shook my head. "That didn't just happen. One of the nastiest people on the planet is over there putting paper cranes under this monument. Cranes that she must have made herself. Unless she rolled some little kid and took them."

As soon as I said the words I wished I hadn't. They weren't funny. And I felt like a jerk taking a shot at somebody — even Lorelei — in this place.

"I take that back," I glanced over my shoulder one more time at Lorelei. Down on one knee, gently setting paper cranes on the sidewalk around her. "But I have to admit I'm surprised."

Zaina nodded. "This is a very powerful place." We moved away from the Children's Peace Monument.

And after we'd walked for a few minutes, I said, "Do you know what time it is?"

Zaina glanced at her wrist. "Just after eleven-fifteen."

"Three-quarters of an hour until we meet Mr. Pettigrew," I said.

"Not really enough time to go through the Museum," said Zaina.

I shook my head. "No."

"Maybe we should just walk around for a bit."

"Sure."

As we looked around deciding which way to go, Zaina said, "Or maybe we should just go our separate ways for a while. Meet up again at noon."

One of the things I had learned about Zaina is that she didn't need for us to be together all the time. Sometimes she wanted her own time and space. And she knew that there were times when I did as well.

I wasn't sure if she wanted a little time to herself right then or if she thought that maybe I wanted be alone for a while. There were times when I was sure Zaina knew what I was thinking before *I* knew what I was thinking.

"Sure, okay," I said. "As long as you're all right with that."

"Totally." She smiled at me. "Go. I'll see you at noon. Don't be late, though, or Mr. Pettigrew will go ballistic."

"Yeah, I know. I won't be late."

I'd never seen Mr. Pettigrew "go ballistic," but there's a first time for everything and I didn't want to be the reason.

Zaina walked off and disappeared into the crowd in seconds.

Now that I was by myself, I wasn't even sure what I wanted to do. But that lasted only a few seconds. Then I realized exactly what I wanted to do — where I need- ed to go.

I walked off at a pretty fast pace because I knew I didn't have a lot of time. A few minutes later I was again standing at the Atomic Bomb Dome. I wasn't sure why, but this was where I wanted to be. To just stand there, looking at what had been a building where people worked and talked and laughed.

And then in a split second — and that's not just an expression, it really was a split second — it was over. Their lives were over. No time to say goodbye or have a thought for the people they loved or to even be sad. It was just over.

Just like it was for eighty thousand others who died in that instant. And thousands more who would take longer to die — but, like Sadako, the girl who made the cranes and whose statue now stood on a monument, death would come to them, too.

As I stood there, I thought about how Anne Frank had made the Holocaust personal for me. And standing there at the Dome, I could see in my mind's eye people sitting at desks, maybe some talking on the telephone, some typing, just starting their day's work. This place — this made it personal. Like Sadako. Like Anne Frank. Both young girls. Both died in the same war.

I looked around. Before when I'd been there with Zaina, there had been a lot of people on the sidewalk, pressing up against the hedge, taking pictures with phones, cameras. Now there was no one but me.

No, I was wrong — there was one other person, a girl about my age. For a second I thought of the girl I'd seen before. But this wasn't her. This girl was Japanese but she wasn't wearing the worn brown school uniform, if that's what it was, and she was older that the girl I'd seen — or thought I'd seen — before.

She was standing as still as the trees that dotted the park. Just standing. Just looking. I could only see her from the side, but her face as sad as any face I'd ever seen in my life.

I watched her for a minute but then looked away, back at the Dome. I didn't want her to see me staring.

A couple of minutes passed and still the girl and I were the only ones at the Dome. I wasn't sure why but

I decided to do something I'm not good at. I've never been comfortable with meeting new people … or with starting conversations with people I don't really know.

But at that moment more than anything I wanted to talk to that girl. I walked over to where she was standing.

"Excuse me," I said. "I don't mean to bother you. Are you from here … from Hiroshima?"

I wasn't sure if she knew any English. When she didn't answer right away I thought she must not but then she nodded her head.

She continued to look at the dome, not seeing me at all. And still the sadness. Complete sadness.

"Was there someone in this building that you knew … back when … it happened?"

Again no answer right away. But this time no nod, no recognition that I was there or that I'd spoken. I turned and started to move away from her, hoping I hadn't disturbed the feelings and thoughts she was having as she stood there.

I was a few steps away when I heard her.

"My grandmother survived that day."

I turned back to her and now she was looking at me.

"Your grandmother was in Hiroshima that day?"

She nodded. "She is a *hibakusha*."

I walked back to where she was standing. "I don't know what that means."

"It is the word we use to refer to the victims and the survivors of the bomb."

"But your grandmother lived? She survived the bomb?"

"Yes, you may say she lived. But in many ways her life was over even though she did not die."

She paused before she said the words *did not die*.

"The life she thought she would have — that every eleven-year-old thinks they are going to have —was gone. Instead she has had a life of suffering, a world without laughter or joy."

"She's still alive?"

The girl nodded.

"It must have been terrible for her … for everyone … right after the bomb …" I hesitated; I wasn't sure what word to use to say what the bomb did.

"I'm sure it was," she was looking at the Dome again. "But my *obaasan* has never spoken of what happened to her that day, or the days after … the years after."

"*Obaasan*," I repeated. "Is that your grandmother's name?"

"No, her name is Yuko. *Obaasan* is the word for grandmother."

We stood then for a while, both of us looking at the Dome, both lost in our own thoughts. Then I turned to her again.

"Can I tell you something?"

She looked at me, maybe deciding what kind of person I was. I was hoping I wasn't creeping her out, that she didn't think I was trying to hit on her. Or that I was just weird.

I watched her as she was making her decision. And when she made it she said, "Yes."

I smiled at her. "My name is Christian Larkin. I live in the United States, but I was born in Canada."

"My name is Harumi," she said.

"There's a bench over there. Would you like to sit down?"

She nodded and we sat on the bench. And for the next fifteen minutes, I told her about Great-Grandpa Will and the Manhattan Project and the protestors at the funeral. And I told her about how I felt guilty about GG Will's involvement with the bomb and how I wanted to do something to make up for it. To make up for him.

When I told her that, I watched her to see if she thought I was strange or stupid ... or both. But her expression never changed. Still there was the sadness, now mixed with ... I wasn't sure ... maybe curiosity.

"It is not your fault," she said softly. "It is not even your great-grandfather's fault. It was war."

I didn't have an answer for that and again we sat for a couple of minutes, not speaking. I knew I'd have to leave soon and wanted to say more to her but didn't know what to say. But Harumi broke the silence a moment later.

"Everything in this park has the word *peace* attached to it — did you notice that?"

I hadn't but as I thought about it now, I realized she was right. The *Peace* Park, the Children's *Peace* Monument, the *Peace* Museum.

I glanced at my watch. I had only a few minutes before I'd have to go. I turned to her.

"Harumi, do you think I could meet your grandmother, your ob ... obsa ..."

She smiled for the first time. "*Obaasan*. Why do you want to meet her?"

I shook my head. "I don't know. I honestly don't know. But it would mean a lot to me to meet her."

"I will have to ask her."

I nodded. "Will you? Could you do that please? We're here for a few more days. I'll come wherever you say. Please ask her. Will you?" I was babbling like a five-year-old in a department store, begging Mom to buy that toy from the TV ad. I knew I must sound pathetic.

She hesitated, then nodded. "I will ask her."

"Great, thank you. How will I know?"

"If you give me a phone number, I will text."

I gave her my number and she wrote it into a little pad she had with her.

"I'm sorry," I said. "I have to go. I'm supposed to meet my group and I'm going to be late."

She smiled again and gave a little wave that was part *goodbye* and part *better get going*. At least that's what I took it for.

"Thank you again so much. I'll … uh … talk to you soon."

And I took off running.

CHAPTER EIGHTEEN

I was the last one there, but I was only about two minutes late. Mr. Pettigrew raised his eyebrows in my direction but didn't say anything.

"I'm guessing you are all hungry," he said. No argument there. "Tomai-*sensei* will lead us to the promised land … well, not quite, but he will lead us to food, which is almost as good."

"Not Japanese, pul-eeze," Lorelei called out.

I looked over at her. She didn't look any different from before she'd been putting paper cranes at the monument. In fact, I was still having trouble believing she'd done that. Maybe I'd been wrong. Maybe it was someone else.

But I knew I hadn't been wrong. Lorelei Faber had been kneeling down and gently placing paper cranes on the sidewalk. And now here she was complaining … again. Hard to figure.

Mr. Pettigrew didn't bother to answer her but Devonne Chelf said quite loudly. "Isn't it weird that here in Japan there's so much Japanese food."

A lot of us laughed at that. Lorelei wasn't laughing.

As we started off after Tomai-*sensei*, I moved along-side Zaina.

"I've got news," I told her.

"*Good news?*"

"I think so," I nodded. "In fact, I'm pretty sure it's good news. I met somebody at the Atomic Bomb Dome and she ..."

I couldn't say more right then because we were surrounded by some of the other kids.

"I'll tell you later."

Later turned out to be after lunch. In the Peace Museum. Zaina and I were standing at an exhibit of items that belonged to some of the victims of the bomb. It was just ordinary stuff, a suitcase, a pot, children's toys, clothing — I guess what made me feel so bad as we toured the facility was that it *was* so ordinary. I've seen lots of baby carriages, but seeing one there and knowing what probably happened to the baby that used to ride in that carriage — that hit home.

"I met a girl at the Atomic Bomb Dome," I told Zaina. "She told me her grandmother was one of the victims of the bomb — that she lived but that she has had a pretty terrible life. I asked her if I could meet her grandmother, her *obaasan*, and maybe talk to her. She said she'd ask her and let me know."

"And what happens if you do meet her, Christian?" Zaina looked at me. "What will that do?"

We turned and began walking toward the next exhibit. "I don't know." I shrugged. "I really don't. Maybe tell her I'm sorry for what my great-grandfather did, for what he was part of. I'm not sure exactly what I'll say to her. I just know it's something I really want to do."

Zaina took hold of my hand. "I know this is important to you. But you can't change history or somehow make this lady's terrible life all better."

I pulled my hand away from her and for the first time I was pissed at her. I was tired of hearing what I couldn't do and that my idea to try to do something to make up for my GG Will's part in what happened was dumb. And even though I knew that wasn't really what Zaina had said, I guess I'd just had it with people giving me advice. None of them had someone in the family who had done what my GG Will had done.

"This is my chance," I told her. "This is a big part of what I came here for. And if I can I'm going to see that old lady. And it doesn't matter what you or Carson or Lorelei Faber think about it, that's what I'm going to do."

It was the first time I'd ever spoken to Zaina like that and I could see she was hurt. I wanted to say I was sorry but right then I wasn't sorry; I was just mad. So neither of us said anything for a while. We continued through the museum, but neither of us was talking.

A few minutes later we came to an exhibit that stopped us both. Inside the glass case was a trike belonging to a three-year-old boy who died that day. The little boy loved his trike and the boy's father buried the trike with the little boy. Then forty years later he dug up the trike and donated it to the museum.

As we turned away from the exhibit, I saw that Zaina had tears in her eyes. I wasn't sure if she was crying for the little boy who loved his trike or because I'd lost my temper a few minutes before.

I took her hand and turned her toward me.

"I'm sorry I was a jerk and —"

But she wouldn't let me finish. "You weren't a jerk and I don't want you to think I don't believe in what you're trying to do. I just don't want you to be hurt if it doesn't go exactly how you want it to."

I pulled her to me and held her for a while, neither of us speaking. We turned and looked again at the trike and a picture of the little boy and his older sister. Then we moved on to the next exhibit, one that had the school uniforms of several students who also died that day. I thought of the girl I'd seen in Tokyo and on the bus the night before and looked for a uniform that was like hers. I didn't see one.

Carson's large face was staring at me from the computer screen. Since our computers wouldn't work in Japan (something to do with the power) none of us had brought them with us. So I was using one of the hotel's computers.

Carson had texted me earlier to tell me that I had to get to a computer and Skype him right away — he had "huge news."

So there he was, grinning at me. Below his face I could see that this particular red sweater was new. It had a giant Mickey Mouse crest on it and below the crest, the words, DON'T MOUSE WITH ME. Even tackier than usual, but I was starting to think maybe that was the point.

I thought about telling him about our day at the Peace Park and meeting Harumi but I decided to save that until I saw him in person.

"This better be good," I said, hoping that the herky-jerky image would still allow Carson to lip-read.

"It's better than good, traveller." He'd started calling me that in our texts ever since we'd left on the trip.

"Nice sweater," I said. "But you didn't have to get dressed up for me."

He laughed. "This screen makes you look even less handsome than normal."

"Ha-ha. What's the big news?"

"Hey, buddy, not just one big news, I've got two news-es."

"News-es? What, did you forget how to speak English while I was gone? Okay, what's the first piece of news?"

"You are looking at a man who has been selected for the ninth-tenth-grade all-star game. We play in two weeks at CenturyLink Field in Seattle and Pete Carroll is going to do the coin toss. Cool, huh?"

I was so excited I almost tipped backwards on my chair. "You're playing in Seattle? That is awesome; that is amazing; that is ... wow!! And Pete Carroll, hey, I'll bet he'll be scouting future talent while he's there. Man, if you were here I'd give you the biggest high-five in history."

"I was hoping you might want to come to the game."

"Are you kidding me? There's no way I'd miss that. Mostly because I want to see you get your butt handed to you in front of thousands of screaming fans."

He laughed. "Have you forgotten who guaranteed the win against Central?"

"Hey, it was the backup place kicker who saved your ass on that one. Seriously, Carson, that is so great. And I'll be there for sure."

"Thanks, now I feel bad about that not-very-handsome remark. You know I didn't mean it, right?" His grin got bigger.

"Shut up. What's the second bit of news?"

The grin disappeared. "Have you got a pen and some paper?"

I looked around the desk I was sitting at. "Yeah, I do. What's the deal?"

Carson had turned serious and I leaned forward so I wouldn't miss what he was about to say.

"Did you ever hear of Leo Szilard?"

He pronounced it *Zillard* and I knew I'd heard or seen a name like that before. I just couldn't remember where.

"Yeah," I said. "I think so. I remember a name something like that anyway."

"Leo Szilard was one of the lead scientists on the Manhattan Project."

I slapped my forehead. "Right. That's where I saw his name. Yeah, so what about him?"

"Okay," Carson looked down at something in front of him. "Write this down."

He recited a website URL. Then he repeated it. "You got it?"

"I got it," I told him. "But what exactly is it I've got?"

"As soon as we're done here, go to that link. Once you're there remember the number twelve. Got that ... twelve?"

"Got it." I wrote that down, too.

"Perfect. Check it out and I would say you're going to owe me for this one. Big time."

"Okay, if it's something really good, I'll buy you a burger at the cafeteria."

He laughed again. This was the big laugh, the Carson laugh.

"Check it out. Text me what you think. I gotta go. I have to pick out my sweater for tomorrow."

"You should try a red one. Be a nice change."

"So long, traveller."

And he was gone.

I got out of Skype and went to the link he'd given me. It took me a minute to understand what I was looking at.

When I finally figured it out, I think I stopped breathing. I must have been like that for a while because I was actually getting dizzy as I read what was on the screen.

The heading at the top of the page read ... A PETITION TO THE PRESIDENT OF THE UNITED STATES.

What followed was a petition to President Harry Truman respectfully requesting him not to use atomic bombs on Japan. The petition was signed by Leo Szilard and sixty-nine other scientists who had been part of the Manhattan Project. I read the words of the petition twice before I remembered the other part of Carson's message, the number "twelve."

And there it was, in the list of the seventy scientists who signed the petition, the twelfth name — William Deaver.

My Great-Grandpa Will hadn't just made terrible bombs to kill people. In fact, he was one of those opposed to actually using the bombs — he was against what happened in Hiroshima and Nagasaki.

I shut the computer down and didn't move for a long time. I thought about GG Will and how hard it must have been to know what the bombs could do and to try to keep them from being used. And to fail.

But he *had tried*. And the best-best friend a guy could ever have, had given me a reason to be proud again of my Great-Grandpa, the hockey-playing prankster who was also a genius. And a good person.

I would have sat there a lot longer but my phone buzzed to tell me I had a text.

I figured it was probably Carson — that he couldn't wait and had to know what I thought of the Szilard Petition.

But it wasn't Carson. It was Harumi, the girl I'd met at the Atomic Bomb Dome earlier that day.

Her *obaasan* had agreed to see me.

CHAPTER NINETEEN

Harumi's grandmother lived in a little apartment above a sidewalk fruit-and-vegetable shop. Tomai-*sensei* had offered to take me there in his car and Mr. Pettigrew had agreed to let me go.

I'm not sure what I would have done if he'd said no, but I was glad I didn't have to face that situation.

It was a quiet ride across the city. I spent the time looking out the window, still trying to imagine what the city must have been like on that day in 1945. The evening's darkness was settling around us when we finally turned down a quiet street that was lined with houses and small apartment buildings, and a few shops here and there.

Tomai-*sensei* parked the car in a little laneway and led the way to *Obaasan*'s building. He told me he would stay down below and look at vegetables while I talked to Harumi's *obaasan*. I climbed a narrow stairwell to the building's second floor. When I tapped on the door of the apartment, it was Harumi who answered and let me in.

She guided me into a tiny, very neat living room. She told me her *obaasan* was just finishing dressing and would be out in a few minutes.

"Thank you for speaking to your *obaasan*," I said. "I'm looking forward to meeting her."

Harumi nodded and smiled. While we waited she told me that her *obaasan* had lived across the street until her husband, Harumi's grandfather, died in 2007. She pointed and through the window I could see a large, square-looking house. Harumi's *ojiisan* (she told me that was the word for grandfather) had run the vegetable stand for many years until his death. Another man owned the shop now, but Harumi's *obaasan* continued to work there just as she had when her husband had been alive. She had moved into this little apartment not long after *Ojiisan* had passed away.

I was about to ask Harumi if her *ojiisan* had been in Hiroshima on the day of the atomic bomb, but the door that I guessed led to a bedroom opened and Yuko-*obaasan* came into the room.

"*Konnichiha, Obaasan.*" I bowed and remained in that position for several seconds, wanting to show the proper respect.

When I straightened I saw that this tiny, frail-looking woman was looking at me in a very kind way. She spoke very softly and Harumi nodded toward an old chair that looked like it was probably the most comfortable one in the room.

"*Obasaan* asks that you sit."

"*Arigatou gozaimasu, Obaasan.*"

Obaasan moved with a distinct limp but still looked somehow graceful as she crossed the floor. She sat on the only other chair in the room. It was as old as the rest of the furniture and looked like wicker or something similar.

In a strange way she reminded me of Great-Grandpa Will, first, because they were both old — and *looked* old — but also because he had this one chair, *his* chair, that he sat in. Whenever I was in the little house in Saskatoon where he lived, he was in that chair. He sat there to read; he sat there to look out the window at the world around him … and he sat there to tell us stories — me, my sister before she got too old for that stuff, and my cousins when they were there.

I suspected that the wicker-looking chair was *Obaasan*'s chair, the one she preferred. And now she sat quietly, her hands folded in front of her, not smiling, but not looking unfriendly or angry. She seemed curious and interested.

I sat down, wondering if the two of them knew that I had already used up most of my Japanese. I was confident with "Hello" and "thank you," but that was pretty much it. I knew more words and phrases but wasn't sure I'd get them right and didn't want to try and end up looking stupid. I'd be okay later when it was time to say goodbye. Between now and then though, my flow of Japanese would be more of a trickle.

But, of course, I wouldn't need to speak Japanese anymore than *Obaasan* would need to speak English. Harumi would translate for both of us.

There were only the two chairs in the room but it didn't matter. Harumi knelt on the floor next to her grandmother. My chair faced *Obaasan*'s chair with not a lot of space between us.

I forced myself not to stare at the terribly scarred part of *Obaasan*'s forehead. And the other scar on the side of her neck. But it was hard not to look. Just as it was really hard not to let my face show what I was feeling as I looked at her. And I wondered if anyone in her whole life had ever looked at her and not seen the scars ... but had just seen the woman called Yuko.

She spoke again, and again it was all I could do to hear her. But Harumi, who was closer, was able to hear perfectly.

"*Obaasan* is wondering what you would like to say to her."

I'd thought about that and practised it a thousand times. And as I looked at her, I said the words that I hoped were enough and that I knew could never be.

"I'm sorry, *Obaasan*, for what happened to you on the day the bomb fell on Hiroshima. I'm sorry that my great-grandfather was part of that day and I am sorry for all the days since the day of the bomb and for your suffering and ..."

I stopped then, partly because the next part of what I wanted to say, what I'd rehearsed over and over, made little sense, even to me. While I thought about how to say it, Harumi spoke to her grandmother, putting my words into gentle Japanese that sounded so much better than what I had said.

When she'd finished, I leaned forward in my chair. "*Obaasan*, I know this sounds foolish, but I was wondering if there was anything I can … do for you. Something you need or something you need done that I could get for you or do for you to … to …"

Again I stopped because what I'd intended to say next was *to make up for what happened and what someone in my family did* and I was afraid that this was the part that was most pathetic. That she would see me as ridiculous or might even be offended by my offer.

And again Harumi translated. And then … nothing.

This time *Obaasan* did not speak, at least not at first. I didn't know what to do … what I should do. Should I say more, try to somehow explain something that sounded lame even to me?

But as I looked at Harumi, I saw her shake her head, just slightly and very slowly, but I was sure I'd seen it. I looked again at the grandmother who was watching me with the kindest eyes I'd ever seen. Eyes that had seen such horror, that had felt such pain … now looking at me.

Then, for the first time since I'd sat down, *Obaasan* turned her head away from me and looked at Harumi as she spoke.

Harumi nodded, then said to me, "*Obaasan* wants to know if you would like tea."

"Yes, I would like some tea very much, thank you, *Obaasan*." I realized I was speaking very formally, maybe to make up for not knowing the correct Japanese response.

Harumi did not translate my words this time. Instead she stood, held up her hand, palm toward me, to indicate I should stay where I was and she left the room.

Obaasan sat quietly, saying nothing, just looking at me. If I was trying to find one word to describe the woman who was sitting opposite me, that word would be *patience*. I think part of that is simply the Japanese way of going through life. But the other part of it was her. I suppose having to live through pain and being scarred and broken and having those things with her since she was a young girl had made her that way. Having her whole life and her home and family taken from her, maybe if she hadn't learned patience, her mind couldn't have taken all that had happened to her. And it too would have broken.

About the time I was starting to feel uncomfortable and thinking that I ought to say something … anything, *Obaasan* reached over to the little table next to her and took a little vase with flowers, small pink flowers, and held them out to me.

"*Sakura*," she said.

"*Sakura*," I repeated. "Very pretty."

"*Sakura*," she said again and then, "pret-ty."

I nodded and smiled at her just as Harumi came back into the room with a little tray and some cups with tea already in them.

She held the tray out to me and I took a cup. When we all had our tea in our hands and had taken a sip, *Obaasan* looked over at the vase and said, "Sakura   pretty."

I explained to Harumi, "*Obaasan* and I have been teaching each other vocabulary in the other's language."

She smiled at me and took another sip of tea.

Obaasan spoke again to Harumi and the grand-daughter looked at the grandmother for a very long time before she translated the words.

"*Obaasan* is going to tell us the story of her life. It is as I told you at the Peace Park. She has never spoken of this to anyone ever before. Ever." Harumi spoke in a whisper.

I turned my eyes to *Obaasan* and watched her and listened to her soft lilting Japanese, then to Harumi's slow, gentle translation.

"It was the morning of my eleventh birthday and I was on my way to wake up my younger brother...."

CHAPTER
TWENTY

"On the way to Kiyoshi's room ... I looked out the window and at that moment there was a flash in the sky. I remember it hurt my eyes terribly and I looked away and put my hand up to face.

"Of course I didn't know what had happened or what the flash was. I did not see the airplane that dropped the bomb. It was only a few seconds until the force of the explosion reached our house."

She paused and took a breath. Remembering.

"I never saw my mother or my brother ever again. My father had been working all night at the shipyard. I never saw him again either. Or any of my friends from school. So many people died. So many disappeared. I thought the world was ending."

For almost an hour *Obaasan* told us the story of the day the bomb fell on Hiroshima. And of the days, weeks, and months after.

Her voice never changed, her eyes didn't flicker. Her expression never flinched, though I know mine did. Many times.

Then she stopped. Harumi stood, picked up our cups, and went to the kitchen for more tea.

When she came back, *Obaasan* asked us if we wanted to eat something, but we both thanked her and said no.

"But what about you, *Obaasan*, are you hungry?" I asked her. "Or do you want to rest?"

But *Obaasan* shook her head.

"There is more to tell," she said. *Obaasan* sipped tea and closed her eyes. But I didn't think she was sleeping or even wanting to sleep. Her mouth twitched slightly once, then again. And I wondered if when *Obaasan* closed her eyes, she was seeing again the terrible things she had seen all those years ago.

She talked slowly and softly, sometimes with her eyes closed, sometimes looking at me — never angry or bitter, not even sad, really. It was as if she was telling someone else's story. Which in a way I guess she was. Because there were thousands of stories like *Obaasan*'s that happened that day.

"I found out that in the days after the explosion my schoolyard was one of the places used to burn the bodies of the dead. It had to be done because of the fear of even more disease spreading from the bodies that were everywhere in the city. I remember feeling sad that the school I loved and the place where I and my friends had played and chattered and laughed was now a place of such sorrow."

She spoke of the months when she was recovering from her injuries and of her return to Hiroshima, the only home she had known. She told us of living in one of the temporary shelters that were constructed throughout the city after the bomb. And how she worked every day, helping with the cleanup ... a cleanup that took years.

She paused then. It was as if she was deciding to tell me the next part. After a minute or two she began again.

"When I became a young woman, I believed that I would never marry. I thought that no man would want someone who ... looked like me even though there were many people who had terrible burns and scars just as I did. For a very long time, many years, I worked at my job as a salesperson in a small furniture store during the day and helping with the reconstruction of our city in the evenings, usually until dark.

"Then one day, a man came into the store. He was short, not much taller than me, and he too was *hibakusha*. But his scars were not visible. In fact, his worst injury was that he had lost all of the sight in one eye and some of the sight in the other.

"I often wondered if the reason he chose me as the person he would share his life with was that he couldn't see me, at least not well." She paused and for a second it looked like the corners of her mouth had turned up just a little. A tiny smile. But a sad one, I thought. The smile of a woman who wanted to look beautiful for her husband ... but didn't believe it was possible.

I remembered the wedding we had seen in Tokyo and wondered what the wedding of Yuko and the man she married was like.

"We married a year later and had one daughter who also had one daughter." She looked at Harumi. "My Harumi-*chan*. This is the happy part of my life."

Harumi smiled at her and I could see the feeling this girl and her *obaasan* shared for one another.

Obaasan had been leaning slightly forward, but now she leaned back, her head resting against the back of the chair. She looked tired and I was aware for the first time of the effort it had taken for her to share the story of her life.

"Will *Obaasan* allow one question?" I said to Harumi.

Harumi translated, then waited. *Obaasan* nodded her head.

"I am very honoured, *Obaasan*, that you have told your story. I was … I was wondering why you chose me as the one to tell what happened to you."

Obaasan paused long enough that I began to wonder if she understood the question or had decided not to answer. Then she pointed at me.

"I know you," she said.

Now it was my turn to sit back in my chair. I didn't know if the surprise I was feeling showed on my face.

"I don't understand, *Obaasan*."

"I have seen you before," she said.

I looked at Harumi, wondering if she had translated correctly what *Obaasan* had said. She must have understood my thought and nodded at me just slightly. I looked back at *Obaasan*.

"I still don't understand, *obaasan*. I have never been to Japan before."

Obaasan nodded and leaned forward again.

"Four months ago, I was working at the vegetable stall. It was a hot, hot day and very busy at the market. All that day I had a feeling that there was someone watching me. After a while I looked up and across the road from the market a young boy was standing looking at the stall. I was sure he was looking at me. He was not Japanese.

"After a few minutes, there came a time with no customers. I looked again and the boy was still there. I walked across the road to where was standing. But I had to wait for a bus and three cars to pass by. And when they had gone by, I looked again and he was gone."

I tried to think of something to say but couldn't find words.

"I saw that boy a few more times, but each time I tried to talk to him, he wasn't there. A few days ago I saw him again. I did not try to talk to him ... but I waved to him. And he waved back to me, then again he was gone."

She paused then and took a small sip of tea, then set the cup down.

"That boy was you. I know that. And when you told me the story of your great-grandfather, I knew why you appeared to me. I knew that you were the one I would talk to of my life."

We sat then, no one speaking. *Obaasan*'s eyes never left my face; it was as if she wanted to know if I believed what she was saying.

"*Obaasan*, I know what you are saying is true. I know that because I have seen someone too. Since I arrived in Japan, I've seen a young girl. She was wearing a brown dress — like a uniform, maybe a school uniform. I've seen her three times, but I didn't speak to her."

Obaasan nodded then spoke to Harumi. Harumi nodded, stood up and left the room. This time she was back very quickly and handed something to the grandmother. *Obaasan* looked down at whatever it was.

"This is the only thing I have left from when I was a girl. It is a picture of me outside my school. It was taken a few weeks before the bomb came. I had it in the pocket of my uniform that morning."

She passed the picture to me. I looked down at it for a long time. It was a black-and-white picture of a happy young student looking at the camera with laughing eyes. The girl in the picture was carrying books and wearing a faded, dark-coloured school uniform.

It was the girl I had seen at the Tokyo airport and at Asakusa and again on the bus here in Hiroshima. It was Yuko. It was *Obaasan*.

The boy she had seen and the girl I had seen — what had seemed impossible. Like ghosts and magic. Things I had never believed in my life. Until now.

I handed the picture back to *Obaasan*.

"*Obaasan*, you have told me about your life, but I haven't done anything for you. I still haven't done anything to make up for what happened to you. And that's something I wanted to do. That I still want to do for you."

Obaasan looked at me for a moment, then leaned still farther forward. She reached out and took my hand. And as she looked at me, I saw again the hint of a smile as she said, "You have done something for me, Christian-*kun*. You have heard my words. You have listened with respect to me. And believed me. And cared. That is enough."

And as I looked at her, I knew she meant it — that this *was* enough … that I had done enough. That I had done what I had come to Japan to do.

"I have one more thing to tell you, *Obaasan*. After the scientists had developed the bomb, they knew how terrible it would be and seventy of them signed a letter asking the president not to use it on Japan. I found out yesterday that my Great-Grandpa Will was one of the seventy who signed that letter. Maybe it doesn't matter, but I wanted you to know."

She was still holding my hands, looking at them. But now she raised her eyes to look at my face.

"Christian-*kun*, this is what I want to say to you. I do not hate the people who made the bombs. I do not hate the people who dropped the bombs. And I do not hate the president who gave the order to use the bombs. War is a great ugliness and terrible things happen and terrible things are done. Your people did bad things. My people did bad things. It does not mean they are all bad people. War is war. And war makes people be something it is not intended they should be."

"But with what happened to you, how can you not be angry?"

"I *was* angry for a long time, but I am not now. I have had many years to think about that day and my life after that day. And I am happy to have had the life I've had. And I am happy to meet the boy I have seen many times before this night. And I hope that boy will return home and be proud of the great-grandfather."

She rose slowly out of the chair and I knew my time with her was over.

I stood up and bowed. When I straightened, *Obaasan* was holding the *Sakura* flower out in front of her.

"She wants you to have it," Harumi said.

"Thank you, *Obaasan*," I said. "*Sakura*."

"Pre-tty," she said.

And then she smiled.

CHAPTER
TWENTY-ONE

It was our last night in Japan.

The days since I had met Yuko-*obaasan* had raced by. But I was ready to go home. I was excited to see my parents and almost looking forward to seeing my sister. And I was totally pumped to see my best friend, to tell him everything that had happened, and hear him joke around ... and even see the latest red sweater.

Our last night. I guess that's why Mr. Pettigrew let us decide what we would do with the final hours of our time in Japan.

And pretty well everybody agreed that what we wanted to do was just what we had done in Tokyo. All of us wanted to walk around the area where we were staying — sort of to take in this country and its people for the last time.

Mr. Pettigrew agreed to let us do that and he even added that he, the parent supervisors, and Tomai-*sensei* would be out on the streets too, but that they wouldn't be *with* us — just nearby. Like they had done that night in Tokyo and again at the Peace Park.

There was something Zaina and I wanted to see. Some other kids too — Devonne Chelf, Jocelyn and Jolene Plouffe, Riley Repp, and a couple of others. We all wanted to go to the Hiroshima Castle. It was a Samurai castle that had been also destroyed by the bomb in 1945 and eventually rebuilt and restored.

It was a pretty long walk from our hotel, but everybody had lots of last-night-in-Japan energy and we got there in maybe a half hour. We climbed to the top of the castle and had an amazing view of the city in all directions — kind of fitting on our last night there. On the way up to the top there were Samurai displays and artifacts, but the best was a display of Japanese toilets through the centuries. There were some fairly crude jokes and we did a lot of laughing.

On the way back to the hotel, we met up with some of the others in the group and everybody wanted to get something to eat. We found the perfect place — actually two places ... an authentic Japanese place right next to a McDonald's restaurant. It was about a fifty-fifty split as to who went where. But you can guess which one Lorelei Faber hit.

It was dark by the time we all got back outside and people drifted off in little groups, all of us working our way back toward our hotel. Zaina and I wandered off on our own. I'd told her most of what Harumi's *obaasan* had shared two nights earlier. But not everything. I hadn't told her about the boy she'd seen ... the boy who she was sure was me. I had decided that was the one part of Yuko's story that I wouldn't share with anyone.

Zaina and I were practising our Japanese. She was still much better than me but I was catching up ... a little. We were pretty into our conversation. Which is maybe why I didn't see the three guys come out of a doorway and spread out across the sidewalk, blocking our way.

They weren't Japanese. In fact, they weren't Asian at all, although they did speak with an accent — I wasn't sure what it was, maybe European.

"We don't like people like her around here," the biggest of the three said, pointing at Zaina.

I looked around and realized it was pretty dark where we were and I didn't see any other students or Mr. Pettigrew or any of the parent supervisors. We were alone. And these three creeps looked pretty badass.

The big guy — I figured he was the leader, stepped forward. "You heard what he said. We don't want her kind around here. We don't ... *allow* ... her kind around here."

As he stepped toward us, he moved into a little more light.

Skinhead.

I figured he was maybe seventeen or eighteen, the other two about the same. I looked at his hands. No weapon, at least not that I could see. Probably didn't think they'd need weapons to deal with a couple of scrawny types like Zaina and me.

We took a couple of steps backward. I'd like to think I'm not a coward, but it didn't take a genius to figure out Zaina and I had no chance against these three. As we moved back, the other two creeps moved up alongside the one who had stepped forward.

So much for no weapons. Both of them were carrying baseball bats. It's funny how your mind works in crisis situations. I remember thinking that with baseball being hugely popular in Japan it made sense that these jerks would be carrying bats.

"So what do you say we just walk out of here and leave you guys be?" I said, surprised that I could get my voice to work at all.

I pretty much guessed their answer before I heard it.

"A little too late for that," the leader said, he was punching his right fist into the palm of his left hand.

I thought about charging the guy and hoping that would give Zaina a chance to get away, find some help, and maybe even get back here before the creeps had time to kill me. The trouble was they had us backed up against a wall and unless I could knock all three of them down, there'd be zero chance that Zaina could get past them. And the chances of my knocking down three guys that were all big enough to play for the Central Raiders were worse than zero.

They took another step toward us. I could feel Zaina squeezing up against me. I was wishing there was something I could do. Anything.

That's when I heard this wild, high-pitched scream. Only it wasn't the scream of someone who was scared. This was the scream of someone who was attacking. And the person who was attacking charged out of the shadows to our right.

It was Lorelei Faber.

She came barrelling toward us, waving something over her head. And, like I said, screaming. She was doing a lot of screaming. She halted her charge about six feet from the skinheads.

"Okay, asshats!" she yelled at them. "Time to move along. We don't *allow* your kind around here."

That's when I saw what it was Lorelei was waving over her head. It was a sword ... a Samurai sword. I had no idea where she'd got it; all I knew is that it looked extremely authentic. And it appeared to me that Lorelei wouldn't hesitate to use it on the first one of the creeps that made a move.

Though Lorelei was pretty round and looked out of shape, I wasn't sure I'd want to mess with her. And I definitely *wouldn't* want to mess with her if she was packing a Samurai sword.

But I guess the skinheads figured a girl with a Samurai sword is still just a girl. And what could she really do? All three turned their attention now to Lorelei. It seemed like their plan was to get her out of the game, then return to Zaina and me.

I took two steps and kicked the leader in a place where guys don't like to get kicked. And, unlike my pathetic effort in the Raiders game, this kick was the real deal. Bullseye. Well, not *eye*, exactly.

He went down in a groaning, puking heap, rolled up in a ball and rocking back and forth. When the other two looked back to see what had happened, Lorelei swung the sword. I have no idea what she aiming at but she hit one of the baseball bats and it shattered and fell to the pavement.

The situation had changed for the three goons. The leader was on the ground and useless, a second guy was now without his weapon, and the third was looking at a wild woman with a sword who looked like she was just getting warmed up.

The two who were still on their feet reached down; each grabbed their leader by one arm and started dragging him back down the street ... away from us. Apparently the dragging didn't feel very good after being kicked in the ... um ... area he'd been kicked in and his groaning got louder.

For several seconds, Lorelei, Zaina, and I didn't move. We watched the three skinheads retreating down the street, then we looked at each other and did something I never thought I'd do with Lorelei Faber. We laughed until our stomachs hurt.

The three of us had turned and started back in the direction we were pretty sure the rest of the group was.

I turned to Lorelei. "I have to ask," I said, "what are you doing here?"

"I sort of got separated from Leah and I thought this might be a shortcut back to the hotel."

"Separated?" Zaina looked at her.

"Well, I guess we had sort of an argument and she walked off and I walked off and we got ... separated."

"Lucky for us," I said. "Where'd you get the sword?"

"There was a booth on this, like, street corner," Lorelei said, grinning, "but the stuff they were selling was toys ... junk. So I asked this one guy who spoke some English if he knew where I could get a like real Samurai sword for my dad." She stopped then and looked embarrassed, like buying your dad a gift was something you should be ashamed of.

"Anyway the guy said he could get me one but he'd need to get it from another location and to come back in a half hour. I did and guess what … swish-swish."

"Swish-swish," Zaina repeated.

"Swish-swish," I said and we laughed again.

I was looking at the sword. "Can I see it?"

She handed it to me. It was heavier than I thought it would be. I checked the blade and it was razor-sharp. No wonder the baseball bat had come out second best when Lorelei had brought the sword down on it.

"Must have cost a lot," I said as I handed the sword back to her.

She nodded, but it was obvious she wasn't going to tell us how much.

"Anyway, thanks for what you did back there," I said. "Things were about to get pretty ugly."

Zaina nodded. "We'd have been in big trouble if you hadn't jumped in to help. Thank you."

"Oh, I don't know," Lorelei said. "That was a pretty good kick your boyfriend got in there."

Lorelei grinned at me and I gave her a thumbs-up.

"That's two amazing things you've done since we got here," Zaina said.

Lorelei's eyebrows came up. "Two things?"

"We saw you putting paper cranes at the Children's Peace Monument. That was so great."

For a minute I thought Zaina might have said the wrong thing, that Lorelei was about to return to being

Lorelei the Terrible. But then she shrugged and didn't say anything as the three of us walked through the streets of Hiroshima.

After a couple of minutes Lorelei said, "I read the story about Sadako before we left home and how she made all those cranes but then she died. And how people come from all over the world to bring cranes to that place. I guess I just wanted to do that, too."

We walked in silence again for a while. I was still trying to get over how one of the school bullies had suddenly showed a side of her that I didn't know existed. Then I remembered how Lorelei had stood up to her mother at the parents' meeting.

I realized that in a way, for both Lorelei and me, there was something we'd had to do in Japan.

"You know how you said all that stuff about my great-grandpa and how he was responsible for killing all those people ..."

She looked at me, trying to figure out whether I was trying to get into a fight or argument.

"Well, you were right," I said, "and I came here wanting to try to do something to make up for it. Stupid, right?"

"I ... I don't know," Lorelei said. "Maybe it's not stupid."

I told her about meeting Harumi and her *obaasan* and hearing the story of what happened to her after the bomb was dropped on this city. And how she'd said that I shouldn't feel guilty about my Great-Grandpa Will and what he'd done. And I told her about Carson's Skype session and finding out about the scientists' letter to the president, urging him not to use the bomb.

Lorelei looked at me and for a second her face had the expression that was usually there when she was about to say something nasty.

But then her expression changed; it sort of softened and she didn't say anything at first. Then she nodded.

"That's really good," she said.

I could see the hotel now. We were just a few minutes away. Lorelei started to laugh.

"What?" Zaina and I said it at almost the same time.

"I was just thinking it might be a good idea if we didn't tell Mr. Pettigrew about tonight, you know, the skinheads and everything."

"You think?" Zaina said.

"Nobody would believe it, anyway." I grinned.

Both Zaina and Lorelei looked at me.

"Okay, so picture this," I held up my hands to present the picture. "It's our first morning back at school and the morning announcements come on '… *and a big Weston shout out to Lorelei Faber who, with the help of her Samurai sword, rescued two of her classmates from some badass skinheads during the recent school trip to Japan. Lorelei will be signing autographs in the Pitt Stop during the lunch hour today.*'"

For the third time that night, the three of us laughed. In fact, we laughed pretty well the rest of the way back to the hotel.

CHAPTER TWENTY-TWO

Things returned to normal pretty fast once we got back to school.

Classes, homework, the cafeteria and mock-shit burgers, and the scramble to get ready for Christmas, now just a few weeks away. Lorelei went back to being Lorelei. She still had the bad mouth and plenty of meanness. I was back to being "Larkin that rhymed with fartin'."

But she never said anything about GG Will ever again. And a couple of times when there were no other kids around, as she passed by me in the hall, she grinned and gave a loud whispered, "Swish-swish."

Oh yeah, and there was the big football game in Seattle. Carson was amazing in that game. And the next day back at school, he was wearing the jersey he got to keep for being on the All-Star team.

It was red.

There was one last thing I had to do. It meant another frantic, frustrating hunt through the tangled maze that was the lower part of my locker.

And, as I had the first time, I found it.

I pulled it from my locker, and headed for the Pitt Stop. I had the place to myself. I selected a table near a window looking out at the football field, pulled out a chair and sat down, dropping my backpack to the floor next to the chair.

I might have been the only student in the school right then. In fact, most of the teachers hadn't arrived yet. I looked at my watch — forty-seven minutes before the first morning bell. I unfolded the piece of paper and set it on the table, running my hands over it, trying to coax out months-old wrinkles.

I read the four words I'd at first thought were so brilliant, then had rejected and now wanted to look at again.

Overhead nothing is speaking

It wasn't much. But I thought about other words that had been swirling in my head during and after our time in Japan.

Time to see if they might work.

Overhead, nothing was speaking
The clouds passed by unnoticed
On earth the birds sat silent, watching
Beauty stopped as if a lens had shuttered
And shattered.
The grass, the trees, held nervous breath
Two women slowly passed

Smoke from distant chimney lifted
Drifted
An anxious cat lay down, then stood again
The tower clock, its hands, reluctant, moved
Ticking to a final stopping place
A resting place
Where time no longer speaks, no more is heard.
The walkers, cat, and birds
Noting the wisp of smoke
Glanced, then higher glanced again
And then …
And then …
And then the sky exploded.

Acknowledgements

A tremendous number of people have been so helpful in making this book a reality. I owe a great debt of gratitude to the Calgary Japanese Community Association and, in particular, its administrator, Mari Sasaki. Special thanks as well to Roy Nagata, Kathrine Nugent, Jerry Kinoshita, Susan Aimoto, Rev. Yasuo Izumi, Anne-Marie Thinnes (who introduced me to Japan); my indefatigable agent, Arnold Gosewich; Shannon Whibbs, who brought intelligence and kindness to the editing of the book; Karen McMullin and the publicists at Dundurn; and, as always, to my family — Mom, Barb, Murray, Kim, Dillan, and Chloe; Amy, Dan, and Gabriella; Brad, Nicole, and Gracie — your support sustains me.

And to the memory of my dad who gave me the most wonderful gift: the joy of reading.

VISIT US AT

Dundurn.com
@dundurnpress
Facebook.com/dundurnpress
Pinterest.com/dundurnpress